The Method

THE METHOD

PAUL ROBERT WALKER

Gulliver Books
Harcourt Brace Jovanovich, Publishers
San Diego   New York   London

Library of Congress Cataloging-in-Publication Data
Walker, Paul Robert.
The method/by Paul Robert Walker.
p.   cm.
"Gulliver books."
Summary: An intensive summer workshop on method acting brings
fifteen-year-old Albie insight on sexual expression, identity, and conduct of life.
ISBN 0-15-200528-5
[1. Method (Acting) — Fiction.   2. Acting — Fiction.]   I. Title.
PZ7.W15377Me   1990
[Fic] — dc20   89-29284

Design by Camilla Filancia
Printed in the United States of America

First edition   A B C D E

To MARLENE,

for loving a writer

The Method

ALBIE JENSEN looked into the mirror as if he were gazing into a dense fog on the coast of Denmark. His voice was deep and resonant. "To be, or not to be, that is the question."

"So what's the answer?" he asked in his regular voice. "And why isn't it working?" Albie had a habit of talking to himself. It wasn't that he was crazy or anything, but sometimes there was nobody else around.

"Too tall," he said, nodding his head in agreement. "People were smaller back then. Hamlet was probably five-four, five-six max . . . no problem." Although he stood 6′3″ in bare feet, Albie had perfected the art of shrinking. He bent his knees slightly and relaxed the muscles in his back. He let his head settle into his spine, curved his shoulders together, and spoke in a small, sad voice.

"To be, or not to be, that is the question: Whether 'tis nobler in the mind . . ."

"Albie, what are you doing?"

Still peering into the mirror, Albie saw the figure of a woman standing behind him in the doorway. She seemed far away, lost in the thick swirls of the Danish fog. It was Gertrude, his mother, the Queen of Denmark.

"Frailty, thy name is woman!" he cried. "A little month, or ere those shoes were old with which she followed my poor father's body—why she, even she married with my uncle." Actually Albie's mother wasn't married to anyone. And, as far as he knew, his father's body was alive and well in Cincinnati.

"Albie, stop that!" Mrs. Jensen ordered. "Turn around and talk to me like a normal person."

Albie took one last look at Queen Gertrude through the swirling Danish fog. Then he turned around and smiled sweetly at his mother. "It's *Hamlet*," he said.

"I know it's *Hamlet*. Stand up straight."

Albie stretched to his full height, towering over his mother. "I'm trying to find the character," he said. "There's a big audition tomorrow."

"For *Hamlet?*"

"No, not for *Hamlet*," he replied impatiently. "For the Company." His mother was okay, but she had an annoying habit of trying to guess what was going on without asking the right questions.

"The Company?" asked Mrs. Jensen. "I've never heard of that."

"It's new. Mr. Pierce is picking the ten best actors in the school. It's not gonna be a big production or anything. Just a workshop. You know—like they have in New York."

"What about the summer musical? You did so well last year."

"Oh, that." Albie sniffed. "Well, of course they'll still have the summer musical. But they let anybody into that—absolutely anybody. The Company is for the *real* actors. The crème de la crème."

"Oh," said Mrs. Jensen, "I see."

Albie looked down at his mother. "What's that supposed to mean?"

"What's what supposed to mean?"

"You know—'Oh, I see.' What do you see?"

Mrs. Jensen smiled and reached up to give him a kiss on the cheek. "Nothing, sweetheart," she said. "I don't see anything. Break a leg."

The audition room was hot and stuffy. Students crowded the walls and spilled into the hallway. Albie sprawled across a plastic chair near the windows. After two years of auditions, he knew that window seats were the way to go—more oxygen to the brain.

Cliff Carlton sat a few seats away, his muscular arm casually draped over Stephanie Wade's shoulder. Albie watched Cliff with admiration. He was so calm, so completely at ease. Of course, what did he have to be nervous about? Everyone knew *he* was going to be in the Company. He'd been playing romantic leads since he was a sophomore.

Albie leaned over to catch Cliff's eye. "Think you'll make it?" he asked sarcastically.

Cliff turned and smiled. His deep voice cut through the surrounding noise. "What you really mean, Albie, is do I think *you'll* make it."

At the front of the room, Mr. Pierce sat behind a small table, shuffling the stack of applications for the Company. His long legs stuck through the front of the table, and Albie noticed that he wore a brand-new pair of hush puppies. His sport coat was draped over the back of the chair, and his tie was loose around his neck. Tiny beads of perspiration glistened along the fine bones of his face.

"Thank you all for coming," he said, looking up from the papers. Suddenly the room was silent. "Unfortunately, most of you will be disappointed. Please don't take it personally. The Company is an experiment. An attempt to give ten student actors the opportunity to develop their talents in six weeks of intensive training. There are many other theatrical opportunities at Wilmont High School. I urge you to take advantage of them."

Mr. Pierce glanced down at the stack of papers. "Jennifer DiPino," he said.

Albie watched the girl step nervously into the center of the room. She was probably a freshman—he'd never seen her before. "Christians to the lions," he muttered under his breath.

The boy beside him whispered into his ear. "Joan of Arc at the stake. The Christians had a chance."

Albie chuckled quietly as the girl began her monologue. Mitch Garfield was always good for a laugh. He was a heck of an actor, too. Not like Cliff, but he was definitely a shoo-in for the Company.

After about thirty seconds, Mr. Pierce cut the girl off. "Thank you, Jennifer. Now I want you to water your plants."

A few students laughed as Jennifer stared at the teacher. "What do you mean?" she asked.

"What I mean, Jennifer," Mr. Pierce said patiently, "is that I want you to *act* as if you are watering your plants. You are an actress, are you not?"

"Yes," she said quietly. "I am." Uncertainly, the girl reached down and pretended to pick up a watering can. Then she moved quickly along a row of imaginary plants, pouring water from the can.

"Thank you," said Mr. Pierce. "I'm sure your plants are very healthy. You may sit down."

As the auditions continued, Albie looked around the room to gauge his chances. He hated to admit it, but Cliff was right—this was a tough one. Ten spots for over eighty students. He did some quick math in his head. Ten out of eighty was one out of eight which was one-eighth which was . . . 12.5 percent. Exactly.

But then you had to subtract the shoo-ins. Cliff, Stephanie, and Mitch for sure. Probably Maggie Llewellyn, maybe Brent Matthews. So actually he was competing with seventy-five students for five open spots. Five out of seventy-five was one out of fifteen which was . . . he scribbled some numbers on the palm of his hand . . . 6.66 percent. Approximately.

But then, of course, you had to compute the talent factor and the experience factor. The talent factor was definitely on his side. It was hard to give it a number, but he deserved at least a three—and that was being conservative. Three times 6.66 percent was almost 20 percent. The experience factor was about 2.5, rounded off to the nearest tenth. After all, the graduating seniors weren't eligible, and he'd been in more plays than most of the sophomores. So that brought him up to 50 percent. Approximately.

Finally, there was the Mr. Pierce factor. That was the hardest to figure. The report cards weren't out, but it looked like he was getting a B+ in drama class. Not great, but not too shabby, either—Mr. Pierce had a reputation as a tough grader. So call that a 1.3 and make it 65 percent. Almost a shoo-in. Approximately.

"Stephanie Wade."

Albie looked up from his calculations to watch Stephanie step into the center of the room. The other boys watched, too. Her honey blond hair bounced lightly off her shoulders, and her hips swiveled with every step. As she turned to begin her monologue, he could see the curve of her breasts beneath the soft material of her blouse.

"He was a boy," she began, "just a boy, when I was a very young girl." Her voice was light and musical, with a sweet Southern accent. Stephanie wasn't a great actress, but she could do a devastating Southern accent. "When I was sixteen, I made the discovery—love. All at once and much, much too completely."

Suddenly, Albie's heart began to beat quickly and his breathing grew deeper. His palms were sweating and his throat was tight and dry. And then—worst of all—the jayster got restless. *That's all I need*, he thought. *The Stephanie factor*.

"Yes, the three of us drove out to Moon Lake Casino," she said, coming to the end of her monologue, "very drunk and laughing all the way."

"That's fine," said Mr. Pierce. "Now, hang your clothes on a clothesline."

As Stephanie reached up to the imaginary clothesline, her breasts became even more obvious under her blouse. Albie gazed in wonder. Then he looked out the window and tried to think about baseball. *Babe Ruth sixty homers in 1927. Maris sixty-one in '61, but eight more games. Henry Aaron 755 lifetime. Lou Gehrig 2,130 consecutive games. Cal Ripkin every inning for five years. Joe DiMaggio fifty-six game hitting streak. Orel Hershiser fifty-nine scoreless . . . Tony Gwynn . . . Don Mattingly . . .*

It was useless. The jayster wasn't interested in baseball. Albie crossed his long legs tightly and tried to keep it where it belonged.

"Thank you, Stephanie," said Mr. Pierce. "Albert Jensen."

Albie sat frozen in his seat, squeezing his legs tighter and tighter. *This is not happening,* he thought. *This is definitely not happening.*

"Albert Jensen," Mr. Pierce repeated, looking directly at him. "You *are* Albert Jensen, are you not?"

"Uh, of course," Albie replied. "You know me, Mr. Pierce."

"We are waiting."

There was scattered laughter throughout the room as Albie slowly rose from his seat. "I'm sorry," he said. "I've got a bad . . . uh . . . back. Very bad back."

"Most distressing, Albert. Perhaps you'd prefer to withdraw from the auditions."

"No. Really. I'll be fine."

Walking like an old man, Albie shuffled toward the center of the room. He straightened up a little at a time, keeping an eye on the problem. *Please*, he whispered silently. *Please don't do this to me*. As he reached his full height, he let out a long sigh of relief. His pants were flat as a board.

"To be, or not to be," he began, "that is the question." He was in trouble from the first word. His voice was cracking, and the Danish fog was still at home in his bedroom mirror. "Whether 'tis nobler in the mind to suffer the slings and arrows of outrageous fortune or to take arms against a sea of troubles . . ." It was getting worse. He had completely forgotten the small Hamlet. This guy could slam dunk a basketball. ". . . and by opposing end them. To die—to sleep—no more."

"Thank you, Albert," said Mr. Pierce. "Now be a salamander."

Albie glared at Mr. Pierce. After all his rehearsals in front of the mirror, *Hamlet* was over in fifteen seconds. "You're kidding," he said.

Mr. Pierce smiled slightly. "I never kid at auditions."

Fine, Albie thought. *Fine. If you want a salamander, you'll get a salamander*. Ignoring his allegedly bad back, he dropped to the floor and pressed his long slithery body against the cold hard tile. His snakelike tail undulated behind him. His beady eyes searched the room for prey. Gum wrappers . . . boots . . . book bags . . . the aluminum legs of chairs. Suddenly he found it. With tiny amphibian hands, he slid across the floor and began to chew on Mr. Pierce's hush puppies.

The students erupted with laughter. "Get him Albie!" "Bite those puppies!"

He was out of control now. He could taste the brand-new suede. He could feel the toes between his teeth. There was no more Albie—just a hungry salamander.

"That will be enough, Albert," said Mr. Pierce, his voice calm and cold. "That will be more than enough."

Albie looked up at Mr. Pierce. The teacher's face was as calm and inscrutable as his voice. "Uh, I'm sorry, sir," he said as he rose to his feet. "I guess I got a little carried away."

Mr. Pierce eyed him coolly. "There is nothing to be sorry about, Albert. Your *Hamlet* was pitiable, but I believe you have great potential as a salamander."

Albie stumbled through his final exams. It was hard to concentrate after the disaster at the audition. According to his calculations, he was practically a shoo-in. Sixty-five percent. Approximately. The Stephanie factor was a distraction, but the real problem was the salamander. What was he thinking? All he had to do was get down on the ground and writhe around a little. But no, not Albie—he had to chew on the teacher's hush puppies.

The cast list for the Company was posted on the last day of school. When he reached the theater bulletin board, a group of students were gathered around the white sheet of paper. Albie stood behind them, reading over their shoulders. His eyes ran quickly over the names. Cliff Carlton, Jennifer DiPino—*good for her*—Mitch Garfield, Maggie Llewellyn—*no surprises there*—Albert Jensen, Brent Matthews, Scott Oker—

"Wait a minute," Albie said out loud. "Wait just a minute." The students turned to look at him. Albie recognized a girl he knew from geometry class. "Would you read that to me?" he asked, pointing to the middle of the list. "Read that name right there."

The girl looked where Albie was pointing. "Albert Jensen," she read. "That's you, Albie. Congratulations."

"Yeah, thanks," Albie said, still staring at the list in amazement. It was undeniable. Crystal clear in cold hard type. The Company. Albert Jensen. There was no mention of a salamander.

ALBIE LOCKED his 12-speed in the trees near the back of the school. There was a regular bike area in the front, with lots of racks and metal bars, but the trees were Albie's special place. It was completely hidden from the sidewalk and the parking lot and the athletic field. Besides, it was closer to the back stairs. Even when the halls were crazy, the back stairs were pretty peaceful.

Mr. Pierce's room was on the third floor, separate from the rest of the drama department. It was once a study hall—now it was a makeshift theater. A stage was built across the front wall, and a musty curtain was drawn across the proscenium arch. Four wooden steps led behind the arch to the wings. The windows were blacked out, and a track of lights hung from the ceiling. A semicircle of ten plastic chairs faced the stage. The rest of the room was empty.

When Albie arrived, Mr. Pierce was stretched out on the apron of the stage with his eyes closed. Albie hesitated in the doorway, wondering what to do. He didn't want to disturb Mr. Pierce if he was sleeping. But then again, it was pretty special to be the first one there for the very first session of the Company. Finally, he cleared his throat and walked in.

Mr. Pierce turned his head slightly and opened one eye. "Oh, hello, Albert," he said. "You're a bit early."

"Yes, sir," Albie replied. "My bicycle was fast."

The teacher closed his eye and rolled his head back to its original position. "That's nice, Albert," he said. "Please take a seat."

As Albie sat in one of the plastic chairs, he mentally pounded himself on the head. *Geez, not only do I wake him up, but I talk like some kind of retard. My bicycle was fast. Right, Albie. Sure.*

After a few minutes, Jennifer DiPino came in and sat down three seats away. She smiled shyly at Albie and looked down at her lap. *I guess sometimes the Christians beat the lions,* he thought. Actually, she was kind of cute for a freshman. Of course she wasn't really a freshman anymore. And he wasn't really a sophomore.

Scott Okerblom was next. As usual, he was carrying his attaché case. Scott was a nice guy and a good actor, but he was so organized it was almost obnoxious. He nodded politely toward Mr. Pierce, who was still lying with his eyes closed. Then he sat down next to Jennifer DiPino and slid his attaché case under the plastic chair. When he was all settled, he turned toward Albie and nodded.

"Albie."

"Scott."

Figures, Albie thought, *he's probably gonna go after Jennifer.*

A moment later, Marla and Leslie waltzed in together. They were best friends, and it seemed like they were always cast in the same shows. Marla was kind of fat, but she was a good actress. Leslie was pretty, if you liked kinky red hair. Marla sat next to Albie.

"Albie, darling," she said with an exaggerated accent, "how *have* you been? It seems like absolutely months since I've seen you."

"Well, I went to Katmandu, but other than that . . ."

Marla let out a long, shaky giggle. "Did you hear that, Leslie? Albie went to Katmandu."

"Glad you made it back," said Leslie.

Mitch Garfield entered the room and sat down on the other side of Albie. He had no idea what they were talking about, but that didn't stop him from leaning into the conversation. "You think you're glad," he said, "I had ten thousand dollars riding on the deal."

Albie looked at Mitch and started laughing. Then he caught himself and acted serious. "We'll talk about that later," he muttered. "Who's the doll?"

Mitch shrugged his shoulders and slipped into his Humphrey Bogart impersonation. "Just some floozy I picked up in a gin mill. She'll keep her trap shut."

Actually the "floozy" was Maggie Llewellyn. Maggie smiled at Albie, and Albie smiled back. He didn't know her that well, but lately she always seemed to be with Mitch. *Figures*, he thought, *all the classy girls are taken.*

Up on the stage, Mr. Pierce opened his eyes and

looked at his watch. Albie glanced at his own watch. It was one o'clock. At 1:03 Cliff and Stephanie showed up with Brent Matthews bringing up the rear. Albie watched them walk across the room and take their seats. Cliff moved so easily—as though he were flowing toward his destination. Of course, it didn't hurt that he had Stephanie on his arm. "The King and Queen," Albie whispered under his breath.

"Yeah," Mitch whispered back, "and Brent's the Fool."

When everyone was seated, Mr. Pierce sat up and swung his long legs over the edge of the stage. For a few moments, he looked down at the students in silence. His eyes were clear and intense. Albie noticed that the chewed-up hush puppies had been replaced.

"You should be very proud," he began. "You have been handpicked for a unique experience in self-exploration. This will be like no other drama class you have taken. All of you will receive A's. I ask only that you be honest, open, and on time." He paused and looked directly at Cliff Carlton. "There are no stars in the Company. Each minute that you are late is ten wasted minutes for the others. Three minutes is half an hour. Six minutes is an hour."

Cliff nodded politely. "I'm sorry. It won't happen again."

"Good," said Mr. Pierce. "I'm sure it won't. Now, over the next six weeks, we will work through a series of exercises. Gradually, we will develop these exercises into a dramatic performance that reflects what we have learned. But the final production is unimportant. It's the journey that matters. Are there any questions? No need to raise your hands."

"You ask us to be open. Open to what?" Scott Okerblom always asked the first question.

Mr. Pierce smiled. "Open to new ways of approaching the craft of acting. Maybe new ways of approaching yourself."

"What about honesty? There's nothing to steal but a bunch of plastic chairs." That was Brent Matthews. He always asked the dumb questions—except he thought they were funny.

"I think you know what I mean, Brent."

"You mean self-honesty," offered Maggie Llewellyn. "Integrity."

"Good, Maggie. Exactly. And that kind of honesty is the most important tool of an actor. Now let me ask a question. What is acting?"

Geez, thought Albie, *let's get down to basics*.

"It's pretending," said Marla.

"Entertaining," said Stephanie.

"Communicating," said Maggie.

"What else?"

"It's playing a role," said Cliff.

"Good, but what else?"

Geez, thought Albie, *might as well jump right in*. "It's being someone you're not."

Mr. Pierce looked at him and smiled slightly. "Good, Albert. You're on the right track. But how can you do that? How can you be someone you're not?"

Albie shrugged his shoulders. "Rehearsal, I guess. Talent."

"Yes, of course," said Mr. Pierce impatiently. "But all the rehearsal and talent in the world will never change you into someone you're not. It's impossible."

"But you said I was on the right track."

Mr. Pierce smiled again, but this time there was a pale sparkle in his eyes. "Because you said the magic word, Albert. Being. Acting is being."

There was a strange silence in the room. Albie felt warm and tingly in the middle of his brain, like there was something pretty interesting going on up there. That was the amazing thing about Mr. Pierce. He could get cosmic in a hurry.

"Being what?" asked Cliff finally.

"Being who?" asked Mitch.

Mr. Pierce jumped down from the stage and paced back and forth in front of the students. Albie had never seen him like this. In drama class he was a pretty cool customer. Now he was like a caged animal. Finally, he stopped and squatted on the floor. As he spoke, he looked directly at each of the students, one by one.

"Being you," he said. "Acting is being you in a way that makes the audience believe you are someone else."

Now he was really getting cosmic. But then again maybe he wasn't.

"You're losing me," Albie said.

Mr. Pierce rose from his squat and stared up and down the length of Albie's frame. Slowly, he arched his eyebrows and lifted his nose as if he had discovered a disgusting bug on his dinner plate. "Poor Albert—he's so tall that the blood doesn't make it to his brain."

There was another silence in the room, but it wasn't

very cosmic. Albie slouched down in his chair and tried to make himself invisible.

"That's not fair," said Mitch. "You asked us to be honest. Albie was just telling you how he felt."

Mr. Pierce looked at Mitch in surprise. "You're right, Mitchell. Touché. Albert, I owe you an apology. And to make it up, I'm going to let you do the first exercise. Be a salamander."

Albie sat up in his chair. "You're kidding."

"Be a salamander, Albert."

"Where?"

"Here." Mr. Pierce motioned to the floor between the chairs and the stage.

Albie stood up, took two slow steps, and knelt down on the floor. *This is too weird. I'm one of the ten best actors in the school, and I'm still a salamander.* He spread his body on the hard linoleum and wiggled his rear end the way he had at the audition. Then he pulled himself along with his forearms and wiggled some more. He could hear some of the students laughing—you couldn't miss Marla's jiggle-giggle or Cliff's HA HA HA. But it wasn't the same. Something was missing. He stopped and looked up at Mr. Pierce.

"That's fine, Albert. You may sit down." He waited for Albie to get settled. "Now tell us what you felt."

"Well," said Albie, "it's hard to explain, actually. There was something missing."

"He didn't chew your hush puppies," Mitch offered.

Mr. Pierce smiled good-naturedly. "And it's a good

thing, too. I can only afford so many shoes on a teacher's salary."

"No," said Albie, "that isn't it. I mean, that's part of it, but there was something else."

"Anger?" asked Mr. Pierce.

Albie thought for a moment. "I don't know. Maybe. But what does anger have to do with my salamander?"

"It's not really the anger—it's the emotion. When I stopped you in the middle of *Hamlet*, you were angry with me. Am I right?"

Albie squirmed uncomfortably. "Uh, yeah. I guess so."

"Of course you were. You then used that anger to bring your salamander to life. That's why you ate my hush puppies and, I might add, that's why you were accepted into the Company." Mr. Pierce paused as if he was waiting for Albie to say something. "Does that make sense, Albert?"

Albie could feel the other students waiting for him to answer. This was definitely getting weird. And the weirdest part of all was that he understood what Mr. Pierce was talking about. "Yes," he said, "perfect sense. Sort of."

"Good," said Mr. Pierce. "Now let's do some jumping jacks."

"Jumping jacks!" Marla cried. "What is this—gym class?"

Mr. Pierce flashed a strange, crooked smile, pulling his lips slightly over his teeth. "No," he said, "gym class is easy. This is the Company."

ALBIE SAT in the bathtub and tried to get comfortable. It was ridiculous. Either his feet went halfway up the tile wall, or his head bumped into the towel rack. Finally, he scrunched himself into a fetal position, with his knees up around his chin. It wasn't good, but at least he could soak his back and shoulders at the same time. The arms and legs were bad, but the back and shoulders were worse.

"Sadistic," he moaned, "absolutely sadistic."

A few quick jumping jacks were fine, but after the jumping jacks there were windmills and toe touches and back bends—lots of back bends. Then there were push-ups, sit-ups, and leg lifts. Then there were wind sprints—back and forth from the stage to the wall. It was almost as bad as eighth-grade basketball practice. No, worse. At least in basketball he didn't have to watch

Stephanie Wade do back bends. He decided to take a cold shower after his bath.

By the time Albie was clean and dressed, his mother was home from work, having a cup of coffee at the kitchen table. "Hello, honey," she said, reaching up to kiss him on the cheek. "How was your big rehearsal?"

Albie frowned in frustration. "They're not rehearsals. They're sessions."

"Well, excuse me."

He grabbed an apple from the counter. "Actually they are sort of rehearsals. I mean we *are* going to put on a production at the end. But it's not really a play or anything. It's just a culmination of our exercises. Anyway, it's the journey that matters."

His mother scrunched her nose like a rabbit. "You smell like Ben-Gay."

"Oh yeah, that," he said, taking a bite out of the apple. "Well, it's pretty funny actually. I was bending over my bicycle and I kind of pulled a muscle in my back. It's nothing really. It'll be gone by tomorrow."

Mrs. Jensen eyed him with concern. "Are you sure? Do you want to go to the doctor?"

"Oh, no, really, it's fine." He gave her a big smile and took another bite of the apple.

"Well, as long as you say so. Listen, honey, I'm going out tonight. Why don't you invite a couple of friends over and order a pizza?" She reached for her purse and took out her wallet. "Here's twenty dollars. Is that enough?"

"Uh, sure . . . thanks, Mom." Albie reached down to take the twenty. "That'll be fine."

"Maybe you need two pizzas."

"No, really. This is fine. I'm kind of tired, actually. I'll probably just watch the game."

Mrs. Jensen sipped her coffee and set it carefully on the saucer. Then she gave him a sad, tired smile. "Why don't you invite some friends over, honey? You spend too much time alone."

He took another bite of the apple. "Really, Mom, I just want to watch the Sox."

"There must be someone you could ask. What about Tommy? You haven't seen him for a while."

Albie sat down across the table. He could tell she wasn't going to make it easy. "Tommy's got a girlfriend. Anyway, he thinks actors are fags."

"Albie! Don't talk like that."

"Geez, it's not a swearword or anything. Besides, I don't care what Tommy thinks."

His mother was relentless. "There must be someone you could ask. Don't you have any friends in the Company?"

Albie stared out into the living room. Actually, that was a pretty good question. He was friends with everybody—sort of. He knew them from plays and drama classes and from regular classes, too. "Sure," he said, "I've got friends. It's just they're not really pizza and White Sox friends. You know what I mean?"

She gave him that sad, tired smile again. "Yes, honey, I know what you mean."

Albie tapped his half-eaten apple on the table. He hated this sad, tired business. It was even worse with the light coming through the kitchen window. It was soft and filtery, and the way it fell across her face really got him.

"Mitch Garfield's been pretty friendly. I mean, he sits next to me, and we always joke around and everything. I guess you could say we're friends."

Mrs. Jensen smiled brightly. "I remember Mitch," she said. "He was in *The Man Who Came to Dinner*. He was Banjo."

"Right."

"Why don't you give him a call?"

"Yeah, maybe. Actually, he's got a girlfriend, too."

His mother shook her head slowly. "Everybody's got a girlfriend except my beautiful boy."

Albie stared down at the table. "I'm not beautiful," he said. "I'm tall and geeky."

"You're tall and handsome. Beautiful and gorgeous, too."

"Yeah, right. You're my mother. You get paid to say that."

"I'd say it anyway." She finished her coffee and glanced at her watch. "Listen, honey, I'd love to sit here and tell you how wonderful you are, but Roger's picking me up at six-thirty. Are you sure you'll be all right?"

"Of course I'll be all right," he said, with a touch of irritation in his voice. "I'm almost sixteen years old." *What's she gonna do—call a baby-sitter?*

Mrs. Jensen got up from the table and set her coffee cup on the counter. The filtery light was already fading, but Albie thought she looked very pretty for a mother. It was just those dumb questions and the sad, tired stuff that drove him crazy. "Uh, thanks again for the pizza money, Mom."

She smiled and kissed Albie on the forehead. "Just remember this—if your old mother can find a boyfriend, anything is possible."

Albie coasted down the long sidewalk to the trees and locked his 12-speed in the secret place. He was still sore from the calisthenics. It was hard to bend over to thread the chain through the wheel. Actually, it was hard to do anything. He dragged himself up the back stairs to Mr. Pierce's room and plopped down next to Mitch, just in time for the beginning of the session.

"Konstantin Stanislavsky," said Mr. Pierce. "C'mon, people, I know you've heard of him."

"Didn't he play middle linebacker for the Bears?" Brent was really reaching for it.

Mr. Pierce smiled slightly. "I believe that was Vladimir Stanislavsky," he said.

Geez, thought Albie. *If I made a joke like that he'd bite my head off.*

"The Moscow Art Theater," said Cliff. "He created Method acting."

"Excellent, Clifford," said Mr. Pierce. "Excellent. Actually, Stanislavsky called it the System. It was Lee Strasberg—a genius of the American theater—who took Stanislavsky's ideas and developed them into the Method."

Mr. Pierce turned away from the students and gazed toward the blacked-out windows. It was as though he could see another time and place in the dark, painted glass. "I was fortunate enough to work with Mr. Strasberg," he said. "When I was a young actor in New York, I was accepted into the Actors Studio. You cannot imagine the creative energy of that place—Bobby De Niro, Al Pacino, Dustin Hoffman, Paul Newman . . ."

"Geez," said Albie, "you knew those people?"

Mr. Pierce looked down at Albie. His eyes were still distant and blissful. "Knew, Albert? Yes, of course I knew them. I worked with them—as fellow actors, fellow artists."

"Wow."

"Why, I remember the first time Al Pacino did a scene at the Studio. He started out as Hickey in *The Iceman Cometh* and turned into Hamlet. From Eugene O'Neill to Shakespeare in the blink of an eye. It was magical."

The students listened in fascination. This was something they hadn't expected—an inside glimpse of the theater world. The way it really was.

"What brought you into teaching?" asked Maggie. "I mean, after acting professionally."

"It was Mr. Strasberg," said Mr. Pierce, looking again into the blacked-out windows. "The day he died, I decided to become a teacher. I left my own career behind." Like a puff of smoke, the distant gaze disappeared, and Mr. Pierce was back on the prowl in front of the class. "Well, enough of that. Let's get to work. Now, today . . ."

"Did they torture people at the Actors Studio? Did Bobby De Niro run wind sprints until he died?" Albie looked over at Mitch and smiled. It was good to know someone else was in pain.

"Poor Mitchell," cajoled Mr. Pierce. "I can see it in the papers . . ." He held out his hand as if reading a headline in the air. "Skinny Student Actor Drops Dead from Exercise."

"People do," said Marla. "You read about it every day."

"I was dying," said Leslie.

"I may never bend my back again," moaned Stephanie.

Suddenly everyone was complaining about the calisthenics. Everyone except Cliff. It wasn't surprising that the exercises didn't bother him. He was built like a rock.

"Okay, okay," Mr. Pierce interrupted. "Perhaps I was a little tough on you. But I wanted to make a point. The body is the actor's instrument. A violinist must tune the strings. An actor must tune the muscles. I look around this room and I see weak instruments, flabby instruments. I want you to stand up for a moment in front of your chairs. Don't worry—I'm not going to flog you."

Mr. Pierce waited until all the students had risen to their feet. Then he passed down the line, staring at each of them as if he had X-ray vision for flab and weakness.

"No more chocolate, Marla." Marla's face turned a deep shade of crimson.

"No more smoking, Mitchell."

Mitch gasped in surprise. "How did you know?"

Mr. Pierce smiled mysteriously and moved on to the next student. Albie waited for the boom to fall. *Okay, here it comes. You are completely hopeless, Albert. Do not collect $200, return to the womb, and start again.*

"Your legs are strong, Albert, but your upper body is weak. More push-ups."

Whew! That wasn't bad at all.

Finally, Mr. Pierce arrived at Cliff Carlton. For a long time, he gazed at him in silence. His X-ray vision checked out every muscle and ligament and sinew. The sandy waves of his hair and the bridge of his Roman nose. The dark stubble on his cheeks and the rugged line of his jaw. It was the kind of stare that would have driven any other student up the wall, but Cliff looked right back. He was completely relaxed.

"You are the only one," said Mr. Pierce finally. "The only one who is ready for the stage."

ALBIE HOBBLED DOWN the back stairs after the session. He was still sore, but it felt good in a strange way. After all, his body was his instrument. Gotta tune that violin.

He passed Mitch and Maggie on the second-floor landing. They were taking it pretty slow. Actually, it looked like they were in the middle of a serious conversation. Albie smiled and walked by. Mitch turned away from Maggie and fixed Albie with a gunslinger stare.

"Chester."

"Huh?"

"You look like Chester on Gunsmoke. Marshal Dillon! Marshal Dillon!"

"Don't make me laugh," begged Albie. "My chest muscles are sore."

"Poor baby," cooed Maggie.

"Hey, you wanta go to Burger Chief?" asked Mitch.

"With you guys?"

"No, with Mr. Pierce and Greta Garbo."

"I just mean, you know, wouldn't I be . . ."

"In the way?" asked Maggie.

"Yeah."

"No," said Mitch.

"Not at all," said Maggie.

It was a tempting offer. The Burger Chief was an old-time hamburger stand a couple of blocks from the school. It looked like a McDonald's, but instead of the golden arches, a giant Indian spanned the building. The hamburgers were juicy half-pounders that stretched your mouth and dripped down your sleeve. The french fries were thick slabs of fresh potatoes, crisp on the outside, soft and scalding on the inside. The shakes were made with homemade ice cream. But Albie's favorite was the onion rings. They were sweet, red, curlycue slices of onion in a light batter that was hardly a batter at all.

"Well, geez," Albie shrugged. "Why not?"

The three of them walked down the stairs and out the back door. It was late afternoon, but the sun was still hot and high in the sky.

"Wow!" Mitch moaned, shading his eyes. "That's one advantage of summer school."

"What's that?" asked Albie.

"Air-conditioning."

"I can see the headline," Maggie declaimed. "Skinny Student Actor Melts."

"Just a minute," Albie said, "I've gotta get my bike."

"Where is it?" asked Mitch.

"Over here—I'll just be a minute."

Mitch and Maggie waited on the sidewalk while Albie disappeared into the trees.

"That looks like a nice bike," Mitch said as Albie rolled it out on the sidewalk.

"It's a Peugeot."

Mitch shrugged. He wasn't really a bike type.

"Do you always lock it in there?" Maggie asked.

"Yeah," Albie replied. "You won't tell anyone, will you?"

Maggie smiled. "No, Albie, I won't tell anyone. Mitch, however, will probably pass out flyers to the entire school."

Mitch shook his head emphatically. "The town. Gotta be the whole town. Maybe the city, too."

"I can see the headline," Maggie said. "Tall Student Actor Hides Bike in Trees."

Albie rolled his bike as they walked over to the Burger Chief. The Chief's headdress appeared as they crossed the railroad tracks. It was pretty bizarre, really. A forty-foot Indian with feathered headdress, war paint, breechcloth, and moccasins. He had a tomahawk in his right hand and a giant burger in his left.

During the regular school year, the Burger Chief was packed with kids every afternoon. Now it was practically empty. Mitch headed straight for the counter and ordered a cheeseburger, fries, and a chocolate shake. Maggie ordered a diet Coke, Albie a large order of onion rings. When the food was ready, they sat down at a red vinyl booth. Mitch dove right for the cheeseburger.

"Pierz gibb be the gree bumtye," he said, trying to talk with a mouthful of food.

"What'd you say?" asked Albie.

"Chew your food," said Maggie.

Mitch swallowed and tried again. "I said—Pierce gives me the creeps sometimes. I mean, how the hell did he know I was smoking?"

Maggie grabbed a french fry and dipped it into the ketchup on Mitch's plate. "He probably smelled it on your breath."

"I always chew gum before rehearsal."

"You still stink."

"Well, excuse me, Maggie."

"I never noticed," said Albie.

"See," said Mitch. "Albie never noticed."

"He's just being polite. Aren't you, Albie?"

Maggie looked at Albie, waiting for him to answer. He'd never really noticed her eyes before. They were beautiful—deep, deep brown with specks of green that seemed to glow in the dark. Of course, it wasn't dark in the Burger Chief—there were bright fluorescent lights all over the place. But they would have glowed if it were dark. He was sure of it.

"Aren't you, Albie?"

"Huh?" He turned away from Maggie and reached for an onion ring. "I'm sorry. I was thinking about something else."

"See, that wasn't very polite," said Mitch. "And what about that 'you're the only one' business? 'Oh, Clifford, you're the only one.' The rest of us ain't exactly chopped liver."

Albie laughed and took another onion ring. "C'mon Mitch," he said, "you gotta admit that Cliff is a great actor."

Mitch set his burger down on the plate and pointed a finger at Albie. "Cliff is not a great actor. He's a great-*looking* actor. There's a difference."

"I don't even think he's so great-looking," said Maggie.

Albie turned to her in amazement. "You're kidding."

"Really," she insisted. "I mean all that hair. And that jaw—a girl could knock herself out."

"You're just jealous," said Mitch.

Maggie pointed to herself in a sweeping theatrical motion. "Moi? Jealous of Stephanie Wade? I may vomit!"

Albie laughed and grabbed a couple more onion rings. "Now you really do sound jealous," he said.

Maggie looked him right in the eyes. Those green specks were really something. "No, Albie, I think it's you that's jealous."

Albie could feel his face turning red. "Me?" he asked.

"C'mon, Albie," said Mitch. "You're not exactly subtle."

"What are you talking about?"

"We see the way you stare at Stephanie," said Maggie.

"Vee see evryting," said Mitch. "Evryting."

Albie grabbed another onion ring and tried to look unperturbed.

"I mean, really," said Maggie, "just because she has blond hair and big boobs, I don't see why every boy in the school has to salivate over her."

"I don't salivate," said Albie angrily. He stared out the window at the Burger Chief's leg. He'd never noticed before, but the giant moccasin stretched right to the edge of the parking lot.

"Hey, Albie," said Mitch, "don't take it so hard. It's just hormones."

"Eat your onion rings," said Maggie.

Albie turned back to his plate and toyed with the food. He didn't feel hungry anymore. "Yeah, sure."

"Want some of my cheeseburger?" Mitch asked. "I can never finish these things. That's why I'm a skinny student actor."

"No, that's okay. I better get going." As he began to get up from the table, Maggie reached out and grabbed his hand.

"Please, Albie," she said. "Don't go yet."

Albie looked down at her. He could feel the pressure of her soft, warm hand. "Sure," he said, sitting down. "I guess I can stay for a while."

"Look, I didn't mean to attack you or anything. It's just . . . well . . . I guess it's none of my business anyway. I'm sorry. Are we friends?"

Albie caught her eyes for a moment. Or maybe she caught his. It didn't matter. Even in the fluorescent lights of the Burger Chief, those green specks really did seem to glow. She was beautiful—there was no doubt about it. Not like Stephanie, but beautiful just the same. "Sure," he said, "we're friends."

"Don't believe a word of it," said Mitch. "She's a vicious bitch, but I love her anyway."

Albie laughed as Maggie hit Mitch with a french fry. All of a sudden he was starving. He decided to order a strawberry shake and some fries. What the heck— maybe he'd even go for a burger.

5

"RELAXATION. CONCENTRATION. MEMORY. These are the three steps of the Method." Mr. Pierce sat on the edge of the stage. His voice was calm and rhythmic, with a new sense of purpose. He was finished with introductions. Now he was speaking from the heart.

"Imagine a room full of gold and jewels." He swept the air with his arm as if the room were waiting in the distance. "This room is a great performance, the goal of the actor's art. Now, how do we reach this room? First we must have the key. That is relaxation. Then we place the key in the lock. That is concentration. Finally, we open the door. That is memory. Each of these steps is necessary. But the key is relaxation."

Albie sat spellbound as he listened to Mr. Pierce's words. He didn't know exactly what it all meant, but that didn't matter. It seemed right, somehow. Right and true.

"When the muscles are tense," Mr. Pierce continued, "it is impossible for the actor to concentrate. Stanislavsky used the example of a man trying to recite the multiplication tables while holding up a piano. You can't do it. It's impossible."

"Why would anyone want to hold up a piano on stage?" Marla asked.

"That's not the point," said Mr. Pierce.

"What *is* the point?" asked Leslie.

"Do you remember your lines from *The Glass Menagerie?*"

Leslie looked at Marla. "I think so," she said.

Marla slipped into the Southern accent she had used as Amanda. "Ah remember everything, sir."

Mr. Pierce smiled. "Good. Clifford and Scott, I want you each to make a stack of five chairs. Everyone else stand up and form a circle in the center of the room. Leslie and Marla will step into the circle and take it from the end of scene two—the "blue roses" business. At a signal from me, Clifford will hand Leslie a chair while Scott hands a chair to Marla. Keep playing the scene normally. After a bit, we'll hand you another chair. Just do the best you can. Any questions?"

Marla looked doubtfully at Mr. Pierce. "Can girls get hernias?"

Mr. Pierce shook his head reassuringly. "Don't worry. You *will* survive."

The students formed a circle while Cliff and Scott piled up the chairs. Leslie and Marla stepped into the circle and began their scene from *The Glass Menagerie*. Albie had seen it before. It was just a workshop production, but he thought they were both terrific. Marla had the desperate dignity of Amanda. Leslie had the fragile beauty of Laura.

"Haven't you ever liked some boy?" asked Marla/Amanda.

"Yes, I liked one once," replied Leslie/Laura. "I came across his picture a while ago."

Mr. Pierce nodded, and Cliff and Scott handed a chair to each of the girls.

"He gave you his picture?" Marla asked. She looked pretty ridiculous holding a chair, but she was still believable as Amanda.

"No, it's in the yearbook." Leslie wasn't as big as Marla, so she had to work a little harder to hold the chair. But she was still Laura.

"Oh—a high school boy," said Marla.

Mr. Pierce nodded and the boys stacked another chair on top of the first.

"Yes," said Leslie. "His . . . uh . . . name was Jim. Here he is in the . . . uh . . . *Pirates of Penzance.*" Laura was gone now. Leslie was just trying to remember the words. "He . . . had a wonderful voice and we . . . sat across the aisle from each other . . . in the Aud. Here he is with the . . . uh . . . silver cup for debating! See his grin?"

Another chair.

"He must have had a . . . jolly . . . disposition." Marla was struggling now, breathing heavily as she tried to hold up the three chairs.

"He used to . . . ummm . . . call . . . Blue Roses." Leslie could barely stand up.

A fourth chair.

"Why'd . . . he . . . uh . . . call you that?" Marla was still hanging in there. It wasn't exactly the right line, but it was close.

Splang!!! Clatter!!! Leslie dropped the four chairs on the floor. "How should I know?" she gasped. "I always thought it was stupid anyway."

"Me, too!" said Marla, dropping her chairs on top of Leslie's. "I mean, who the hell cares?"

The students laughed as they dodged the tumbling chairs. After the chairs had settled, Mr. Pierce stepped into the circle. "Bravo!" he said, clapping his hands. "Bravo! You lasted longer than I expected." He looked at the two girls with concern. "I trust there are no hernias."

Marla took a deep breath. "I'm fine," she said.

"I'll live," said Leslie.

"Good," said Mr. Pierce. "Now, tell us what you learned."

Leslie thought for a moment. "I learned that I never want to do *The Glass Menagerie* while holding four chairs."

"But you could do it holding one chair," said Mr. Pierce.

Leslie brushed her hair off her forehead. "I suppose," she said. "I mean, it's kind of stupid but, yes, I think I could do it."

"Now, what's the difference between one chair and four chairs?"

"Three chairs," said Brent.

"No," said Mr. Pierce, "the difference—for the actor—is muscle tension. You cannot play the part because of the muscle tension it requires to hold the additional chairs. Let's take it further. An actor steps onto the stage. He must be aware of everything—his own role, the other roles, the vision of the director, the intent of the playwright, the setting, the props, the lights."

"That's a lot to think about," said Maggie.

"Yes, it is," said Mr. Pierce. "But he is not just thinking. Thinking will only get in the way. No, the actor must concentrate. He must be completely aware. Now, perhaps he had a fight with his girlfriend. Or maybe he drove through a traffic jam on the way to the theater. Whatever the reason, he is carrying tension in his body. He cannot possibly concentrate at the level necessary for a great performance."

"So what does he do?" asked Albie.

Mr. Pierce smiled. "He drops the chairs, Albert. Do you understand?"

Albie looked down at the floor. "Uh, sort of. I mean, more or less."

Mr. Pierce stood directly in front of him. "Look at me, Albert," he ordered. "If I gave you one minute to observe my clothing, could you close your eyes and tell us everything you saw?"

"Uh, sure. I mean, I think so."

"Let's try it. Remember, you must notice everything. Are you ready?"

"Ready."

"Begin."

Albie's eyes focused on Mr. Pierce's sport coat, shirt,

and tie. Then he moved on to his belt and pants. Finally, he checked out his shoes and socks. *This is easy. What's the big deal?* There was still plenty of time left, so he did it all again. No problem. He had it down pat.

"Time," said Mr. Pierce. "Now close your eyes and tell us what you observed."

"Well," said Albie, "you're wearing a blue sport coat and a yellow shirt. Your tie is, uh, sort of pink with little blue flowers. Your belt is black and your pants are white. You're wearing dark blue socks and black hush puppies." It was funny—as soon as he closed his eyes, the pictures began to fade. But he was still sure he had it all right.

"You may open your eyes."

Right away, Albie knew he was in trouble. Mr. Pierce was smiling at him like a cat watching a canary.

"What'd I miss?" Albie asked.

"You tell me," said Mr. Pierce. "But first I want you to relax. All of you—lie down on the floor. Albert is not the only one with too many chairs."

As the students spread out on the floor, Mr. Pierce stepped to the side of the room and dimmed the lights. "There, that's better. Much better." His voice was different—warmer and kinder. "Comfortable? Good. I want you to be comfortable. Loose . . . completely loose."

Now his voice was like water running gently in a mountain stream. "First you let go of your feet. Your right foot is totally relaxed. Even your toes. Now your left foot and toes. Totally loose and relaxed. Now your legs. Your right calf, then your left calf. Your thighs. Your right thigh. Your left thigh. Completely relaxed . . . no tension whatsoever. Now your genitalia.

No need to laugh—you've all got genitalia. Let it go. Let everything go below the waist. Empty and loose and relaxed."

Albie felt the tension in his body disappearing as he listened to Mr. Pierce's commands. It was amazing. He really was loose and relaxed below the waist.

"Now your abdomen and your lower back. Completely loose . . . no tension whatsoever. Let it go. Let it all go. Your chest and your upper back. Your shoulders, your arms. First your right arm—the bicep, the elbow, the forearm, the wrist . . . completely relaxed . . . the hand, each finger, one by one . . . loose and relaxed. Now your left arm . . . completely relaxed and limp . . . you have no tension whatsoever. Now your neck. It is completely loose. Your head flops like a rag doll on the floor."

Albie's head flopped from side to side. "I am soooo looooose," he mumbled.

"Quiet, Albert. Relax your jaw and the muscles in your face. Let them go completely—the muscles around your mouth, your nose, your eyes and your temples, your forehead, even the tension in the top of your skull . . . all of it is completely gone. You are completely loose . . . limp from head to toe . . . like a rag doll lying on the floor."

Slowly, the light grew brighter. Mr. Pierce stepped into the midst of the students. "All right," he said, "sit up and rest for a few moments. When you're ready, you may gradually rise to your feet. Stand straight and strong without tension. Well, Albert, what am I wearing?"

Albie looked at Mr. Pierce. At first it was hard to

focus—he was too relaxed. Then the details began to emerge. It was as if he were looking at Mr. Pierce for the first time. "Your sport coat is striped. I mean they're just little stripes—pinstripes, I guess. And your shirt isn't yellow, it's gold. And the blue flowers on your tie— they're wheels. Little black wheels."

Mr. Pierce broke into a wide smile. "Excellent, Albert! Excellent! What else do you see?"

"Your pants—they're not white. They're more like beige, with tiny colored specks."

"Quite dapper, aren't they? What else, Albert? Not just colors."

"Uh, geez."

"What about my shoes? Are they really hush puppies."

Albie stared at the teacher's shoes. All of a sudden it was hard to focus. "They look like hush puppies," he said. "Sort of."

Mr. Pierce raised his right foot and rested it on an overturned chair. "Look, Albert. Look!" he shouted. "They are not hush puppies. They have soft, black leather tops with black crepe soles—they're just glorified gym shoes. You thought they were hush puppies because I usually do wear hush puppies. One careless glance was enough to convince you of something that was false."

"Geez. I'm sorry."

"Don't be sorry, Albert. Be aware."

"C'mon," said Mitch, "not even a trained actor would notice everything."

"Yes, Mitchell, he would. Or at least he could."

"Like the thumbtack in your heel," said Cliff.

Mr. Pierce raised his shoe to look at the heel. "Exactly, Clifford. And what does that tell you?"

Cliff thought for a moment. "It tells me that you've been walking near the theater bulletin board."

"Excellent, Clifford. Your powers are growing." Mr. Pierce looked at the other students. "What else do you see?"

"The large ring of keys on your belt," said Maggie. "It tells me that you're a man of responsibility."

"The dust on the seat of your pants," said Scott. "It tells me you've been sitting on the stage."

"The cut on your neck," said Stephanie. "You shaved in a hurry."

"Excellent!" cried Mr. Pierce, almost laughing with joy. "Excellent! All of you."

"Geez," Albie said, "you make it seem like an actor should be a detective."

"Exactly," said Mr. Pierce, his face turning serious. "A detective solving the mystery of life."

MITCH LEANED BACK against the Jensens' couch and made a face like an overstuffed pig. "Ohhh," he moaned, "I am going to die."

"Idiots!" Albie screamed at the television. "Complete idiots! They've got a man on second with no outs, and they hit to the left side. Pass the pizza, willya Mitch?" It was the second week of sessions, and the exercises were getting intense. It felt good to unwind.

Mrs. Jensen stepped into the living room from the kitchen. She was dressed to go out. "If you boys are still hungry," she said, "there's pasta salad in the fridge and chocolate cake for dessert."

"Oh, no, Mrs. Jensen," Mitch pleaded, "really, I can't eat another bite."

She eyed Mitch doubtfully. "You're too skinny, Mitch. Why, in *The Man Who Came to Dinner* you practically disappeared when you turned sideways. I kept saying, 'Where's Banjo? What happened to Banjo?' "

"Don't make me laugh," Mitch begged, laughing despite himself. "The pizza doesn't like it."

"Well, suit yourself," said Mrs. Jensen. "I can't force you. Albie, why are you staring at me like that?"

Albie continued to stare at his mother.

"Stop that, Albie. It's not polite."

"You dyed your hair," Albie said. "And you dressed in a hurry."

Mrs. Jensen touched her hair nervously. "What are you talking about?"

"I know you dyed your hair, because there's a small brown smudge on the left side of your neck just below the hairline. I know you dressed quickly because there's a run in your right stocking. Normally you would notice the run and change your stockings."

Mrs. Jensen glanced down at her right leg. "Well!" she exclaimed. "I didn't know I was living with a private investigator."

"He's investigating the mystery of life," said Mitch.

Mrs. Jensen looked at Mitch strangely. "What?"

"The mystery of life," Albie repeated. "It's from the Company."

"That Company," she said. "Sometimes I think you're all completely crazy."

"We are," said Mitch, contorting his face into the features of a maniac. "Completely. Heh! Heh! Heh!"

Mrs. Jensen jumped slightly at the sound of a horn on the street below. "Darn!" she said. "That's Roger. We're already late. What am I going to do about this stocking?"

Albie grabbed the paper napkin from his plate, stood up, and walked toward his mother. "Forget the stocking," he said. "Just let me wipe this hair dye." He spit on the napkin and cleaned up the brown smudge. "There, that's better. Now get outta here."

Mrs. Jensen stood in the living room, still trying to make up her mind. The horn sounded again from the street.

"You look great," Albie said. "Roger won't be looking at the back of your stockings." He drew himself up to his full height and spoke in the deep tone of a stern father. "At least he'd better not be looking there, young lady."

Mrs. Jensen blushed and grabbed her evening bag. "Oh, Albie . . . Good night, Mitch."

"Good night, Mrs. Jensen. Thanks for the pizza."

"Anytime. You're always welcome here."

Albie watched as his mother walked out the door. "I expect you home by midnight," he called.

"She's a nice lady," said Mitch.

"Yeah, she's all right." Albie grabbed another piece of pizza and sat down in front of the television. "I can't believe these guys. They stink! A lead-off double and they can't get him in."

"I don't know much about baseball," said Mitch.

Albie turned to look at him. "Weren't you in Little League?"

Mitch shook his head. "Naw. Well, actually, I was in Pee Wee League for a while, but I kept throwing to the wrong base."

Albie sat silently for a moment, watching the television. It was hard to imagine someone who couldn't play baseball.

"I like track, though," Mitch continued. "I ran the 220 my freshman year."

"Wow! We're the exact opposite. I can hit a baseball a mile, but it takes me six hours to run the bases."

Mitch smiled and shrugged. "Different strokes for different folks."

"One time the coach put in a pinch runner while I was rounding second," Albie said. "That's how slow I am."

Mitch laughed and let out a long, slow belch, "Burrrrp! Oops, sorry about that."

"No problem." Albie took another bite of pizza. He chewed slowly, studying Mitch out of the corner of his eye. It was funny—they talked all the time at school, but not like this. "Hey," he said casually, "you want a shot of whiskey or vodka or something?"

Mitch leaned forward in surprise. "I guess so. I mean if you do."

Albie tossed his head confidently. "Why not? I do it all the time." He set his half-eaten pizza back down on the plate. "Well, actually, I never do it, but I could do it anytime I wanted to. My mom keeps a whole bunch of liquor in the cabinet next to the refrigerator. It's for company." Albie thought for a moment. "Hey, you're company! Aren't you?"

"Definitely," Mitch replied.

"And you're practically eighteen."

"Well, actually, I just turned seventeen last month. But I suppose you could call that practically eighteen."

"And eighteen used to be legal drinking age in Wisconsin."

"And we're practically in Wisconsin," Mitch said. He was getting the hang of this.

"So it wouldn't be wrong to offer you a drink."

"Not at all."

"And it would be rude to let you drink alone."

"Absolutely."

"So what'll it be, whiskey, scotch, or vodka?"

"Whiskey."

"Whiskey it is." Albie jumped to his feet and headed for the kitchen. He opened the top cabinet, reached over the regular glasses, and carefully removed two shot glasses. Then he knelt down and opened the liquor cabinet. Once again he was very careful as he reached around the other bottles and removed the whiskey.

"Like a cat burglar," he said aloud as he closed the cabinet. "Just like a cat burglar." Rising to his feet, Albie poured two perfect shots of whiskey. He carried them into the living room, handed one to Mitch, and raised the other in a toast. "To the Company!"

Mitch raised his shot glass and looked directly at Albie. "No," he said. "To friendship. Thanks for inviting me."

Albie smiled and looked into Mitch's eyes. "To friendship," he said. Then he tossed the shot down his throat. It was warm and mellow as it slid along the esophagus, but it hit his stomach like a forest fire. "Wow! This stuff is intense," he gasped, coughing and trying to catch his breath. "People actually like this?"

Mitch smiled as he handed Albie his empty shot glass. "It takes practice," he said.

"Well, what the hell, let's practice some more." Albie walked back into the kitchen and poured two more shots. The forest fire was calming down a little, and everything had a nice hazy glow. He spilled a little whiskey on the counter, but he wasn't worried. He could clean it up later.

When Albie returned to the living room, Mitch was watching the game again. "Idiots!" he yelled. "They keep throwing to the wrong bases. I shoulda stayed in Pee Wee League."

"Don't make me laugh," said Albie. "I'll spill the whiskey." Very carefully, he handed Mitch a shot glass and held his own glass out for the toast. "To the Company!"

Mitch laughed. "All right. To the Company!"

The two boys threw their shots down. Albie felt the liquor slide all the way down to his stomach. He waited for the forest fire, but it was more like a backyard barbecue. "Hey," he said, "this stuff isn't bad at all. One more time?"

"Naw, I don't think so."

Albie stared at the television. There was a wide-angle shot of an empty baseball diamond. "What happened to the game?" he asked.

"It must be over," said Mitch.

"Who won?"

"Who knows?"

"Who cares? They're just a bunch of bums."

"Right," said Mitch, "a bunch of no-good bums who throw to the wrong bases."

Albie turned away from the television and stared at Mitch. "I think you're drunk," he said.

"I think you're drunk."

"I don't feel drunk."

Mitch held up one finger very seriously. "That's the first sign."

Albie stepped over the pizza and turned off the television. "So what do we do now?" he asked.

Mitch glanced at his watch. "I better get going."

"What time is it?"

"Quarter to ten."

"It's still early."

Mitch put his hand behind his head and posed like a Hollywood glamour queen. "I need my beauty sleep, darling."

Albie laughed. "You're weird, Garfield. Really weird. I'll walk you home."

"Sure."

Albie glanced toward the kitchen. The whiskey bottle stood like a lonely sentinel on the counter. "One for the road?" he asked.

"I don't think so."

"C'mon," said Albie. "We'll drink to Maggie."

"Won't your mother notice?"

Albie shook his head. "Don' worry about her. I'll pour a lil' water in and stick the bottle in the back. C'mon. To Maggie."

Mitch shrugged his shoulders. "Okay. But just one."

Albie picked up the shot glasses and walked into the kitchen. The haze was really beautiful now, and the whiskey bottle was smooth and solid in his hand. It was tough to get the liquor into those goddamn little glasses, though. He kept spilling it on the counter. Finally, he was all set, and he carried the shots out to Mitch.

"Here y'go, Mitch, buddy. One lil' shot for the road." Solemnly holding his shot in the air, Albie began the toast. "To Maggie! A nice girl with some green sparks and a pretty good body to boot."

Mitch shook his head. "To Maggie! A beautiful lady."

"I'll drink to that." Albie tossed the shot down and smiled as it hit his stomach. No forest fire. No barbecue. Just a nice whiskey glow.

The night was warm and pleasant, with a slight breeze blowing off the lake. There was no moon, and the old-fashioned streetlamps cast hazy pools of light across the sidewalk. Albie's neighborhood was mostly redbrick apartment buildings or boxy four-flats. Mitch lived a few blocks to the north, where older houses began to mix with the apartments. The houses weren't fancy, but some of them went back to the turn of the century.

Albie took a long, deep breath of the summer breeze. "These nights make me crazy," he said.

Mitch smiled. "I think you're crazy to begin with."

Albie gave Mitch a friendly shove. "Oh, yeah, like you're Mr. Normal." The shove wasn't much of anything, but Albie was so much bigger than Mitch that he knocked him off the sidewalk.

"I never said that," said Mitch, stepping back onto the sidewalk.

"Sorry," Albie said. "I didn't mean to push you . . . so hard." He was having some trouble with his words.

Mitch shrugged and smiled. "That's okay."

The two boys walked for a while in silence. Albie thought about Maggie. She really was beautiful. Green sparks, good body. The whole package.

"So are you doin' it?" he asked.

Mitch stopped to look at him. "Huh?"

"Are you doin' it? You an' Maggie. Are you getting it on? Y'know — givin' it to her."

Mitch stood absolutely still. It was hard to read his eyes in the dim light from the streetlamps, but Albie could tell he was angry. "You shouldn't talk like that," he said. "It's not right."

"Whadya mean?" Albie asked. "We're friends aren't we? Friends talk about everything."

"What about Maggie? Isn't she your friend?"

Albie thought for a moment. Maggie was pretty friendly for a girl, but he couldn't picture her eating pizza and watching baseball. Not to mention drinking whiskey. "Geez," he said. "Yeah, sure. But it's not like us. I mean we're guys."

"Yeah," said Mitch. "We're guys all right. Just leave Maggie out of it." Without waiting for Albie to answer, he turned away and started walking again, faster than before. With his long legs, Albie had no problem keeping up, but he was surprised by Mitch's anger. *So he's not doin' it. So what? At least he's got a girlfriend.*

They were almost to Mitch's house when Mitch turned down a little gravel alleyway that ran behind some of the old wooden buildings.

"Where we going?" Albie asked.

"C'mon," said Mitch. "I wanta show you something."

Albie followed Mitch down the alleyway. There were no streetlamps. He could hear Mitch's feet kicking and scraping on the gravel and he could dimly see the form of his skinny body moving against the darkness. Suddenly, the sound of the gravel disappeared, and Albie could feel grass under his feet. After a few more steps, Mitch turned to face him.

"Well, what do you think?" he asked.

Albie looked around at the darkness. "What is it?" he asked.

"My place," said Mitch. "This is where I come when I want to think."

As Albie's eyes slowly adjusted to the darkness, the shapes around them materialized. It was almost magical—as if they came out of nowhere. There wasn't much. A swing set . . . teeter-totters . . . a sand box. That was it.

"It's a park," said Albie. "For little kids."

Mitch sat down on one of the swings. "The smallest park in town. Nobody ever comes here."

Albie sat down on the swing beside him. "So, whaddya think about?"

Mitch pushed off from the ground and began swinging back and forth. "Lots of things. The meaning of life—y'know, stuff like that."

Albie pushed off and pumped his legs out and in, building speed until he was even with Mitch. It felt a little weird with the whiskey but it was fun. He hadn't swung in years. "Seriously," he said, "whaddya think about?"

Mitch pumped harder, and soon he was swinging in the highest possible arc. Albie did the same. The swing set was jumping a little. It wasn't made for big boys.

"The White Sox," Mitch said. "Mostly I think about the White Sox."

Albie laughed hard. He could feel the whiskey and pizza sloshing around inside. He let his long legs dangle, shortening his arc. After a moment, Mitch slowed down, too. Now they were just swinging comfortably side by side.

"What about the Company?" Albie asked. "You seem kind of down on it."

"Naw, I'm not down on it," said Mitch. "Sometimes I just don't have the patience."

"Don't you want to be an actor?"

"I don't know. I thought I did." Mitch let his legs dangle until he came to a stop. Albie did the same.

"But you've got so much talent," Albie said.

Mitch turned to look at him. "Talent? What kind of talent?"

"Geez, I think you're the funniest guy in the school."

Mitch reached into the right pocket of his pants and took out a crumpled packet of cigarettes and a book of matches. He slipped a cigarette out of the pack and stuck it in his mouth. "Oh, I'm funny all right," he said. "I'm a regular laugh-riot."

"I thought you quit," said Albie.

Mitch lit his cigarette and took a long, deep drag.

He held it in his lungs for a moment, and slowly exhaled the smoke into the darkness. Then he crammed the pack and the matches back into his pocket. "I'm trying to," he said, taking another drag on the cigarette. "But it isn't easy."

The two boys sat together in silence. Albie could still feel the whiskey working in his blood. It was hard to see the hazy glow in the darkness of the little park, but it was there just the same. Only now it wasn't so beautiful. It was mellow and slow and maybe kind of sad. The sadness came from Mitch. Albie could hear him breathing beside him. He could smell his tobacco in the hot summer air. But he couldn't understand the sadness.

"I'm a gym shoe!" Mitch cried suddenly. "I'm a goddam' glorified gym shoe!"

Albie turned to look at him. "What are you talking about?"

Mitch took another drag on the cigarette. He was excited now. "Mr. Pierce was wearing black gym shoes, but you thought he was wearing hush puppies because he usually does wear hush puppies. You remember?"

"Yeah," said Albie. "Of course I remember."

"Well that's me! I'm a glorified black gym shoe, but everyone thinks I'm a hush puppy—because I used to be a hush puppy."

"You're drunk."

"Maybe," said Mitch, his voice suddenly drained of emotion, "but I don't think so. Maggie doesn't think so, either."

"What's Maggie got to do with it?"

"She listens. She sees the change."

"I'm listening."

Mitch took a last drag on his cigarette and flicked the butt into the dirt at his feet. He watched it burn for a moment and ground it out with the tip of his boot. "You're listening," he said seriously, "but you're not hearing."

7

BAM! BAM! BAM! BAM!

Albie stared at the ceiling of his bedroom. There was a long, thin crack running directly overhead.

Bam! Bam! Bam! Bam!

"Ohhhhhh," he moaned. "It feels like hammers inside my head."

Bam! Bam! Bam! Bam!

Suddenly the crack in the ceiling disappeared, and Albie was staring into the face of his mother.

"I hope you're proud of yourself," she said.

"They're hammering in my head."

"I'll show you hammering." Mrs. Jensen leaned directly over his face. "You smell like a distillery."

"Ohhhhhh," he moaned. "Tell them to stop hammering. Please, Mom."

"Don't you 'Please, Mom' me. You drank enough

whiskey for a battalion." The crack in the ceiling reappeared, but Albie could still feel her standing beside his bed.

"But it was just a few shots," he said.

"A few shots my eye. Half the bottle's gone."

"Mitch had some."

"I'm sure he did. But Mitch is not my son, and Mitch is not lying in front of me moaning like a dying animal."

"Ohhhhhh," he moaned, "I *am* a dying animal."

"We'll discuss this later," said Mrs. Jensen. "I'm already late for work." Albie felt her walk away from his bedside. Kaboom! The door of his room slammed like a hydrogen bomb.

Albie stared at the crack in the ceiling and tried to remember. He and Mitch had three shots each. It was a lot, but it wasn't half a bottle. He could remember sitting with Mitch on the swings of the little park and talking about gym shoes and hush puppies. He could remember saying good night and walking home. He could even remember feeling kind of sad and empty and alone. But that was it. Everything else was blank.

Albie closed his eyes and curled up into a ball. The hammers were still pounding in his head, but he felt very tired. *Let them hammer in my dreams.*

When he woke up, the hammers were gone, but his tongue tasted like the Kalahari Desert. "Water!" he whispered. "Give me water!"

He opened his eyes and rolled out of bed. The room was hot and full of sunlight. His bedroom was always cool and dark in the morning. That was the best thing about it. The windows faced west, so the sun never hit it until the afternoon. Afternoon! Albie glanced at the clock on his dresser. It was 1:03. He was already late.

"Shit!" He threw on a pair of cut-offs, a T-shirt, and some tennies. Then he ran into the bathroom, splashed some water on his face, and drank directly from the faucet. When he came up for air, he looked at his face in the mirror. His eyes were bloodshot with deep dark circles beneath them. His entire face was swollen. It looked like a bad make-up job.

"I am dead. Dead meat."

He ate half a tube of toothpaste and ran into the kitchen. The whiskey bottle was standing on the counter like a hanging judge. There was a pool of brown sticky liquid around it. The whole kitchen stank.

"Blchhhh!"

He opened the refrigerator, grabbed a wad of bologna, and stuffed it in his mouth. As he chewed the bologna, he ran out of the apartment and down to the basement. He unlocked his bicycle, carried it up the basement steps, and walked it out to the street. Then he hopped on and rode up the hill toward the high school. Normally, it was a twenty minute ride, but if he really cranked he could make it in fifteen.

Twelve minutes later, he was outside the school. He didn't have time for his special place, so he locked his bike in the racks and ran in the front door. He kept on running up the front stairs and down the third-floor hallway to Mr. Pierce's room.

As soon as he opened the door, he knew it was serious trouble. Mr. Pierce was sitting on the edge of the stage, looking at his watch. The rest of the students were sitting in their chairs, doing nothing. Absolutely nothing. Not talking. Not stretching. Not relaxing. Not concentrating. Nothing.

"Albert," said Mr. Pierce, "how kind of you to grace us with your presence."

Albie stood in the doorway. His T-shirt was drenched, and sweat was dripping down his face. He was breathing hard. "I'm sorry, sir," he said. "I . . . overslept."

Mr. Pierce looked at his watch. "It is now one-twenty-one. You are twenty-one minutes late. Ten of us have been waiting for twenty-one minutes. Ten times twenty-one is two hundred ten. Thus you have cost the Company two hundred ten minutes or three and a half hours. In view of this unfortunate waste of time, I think it would be best if we cancel today's session and try again on Monday." With that, Mr. Pierce slid off the stage and walked out of the room. He brushed past Albie as if he didn't exist.

This is a dream, Albie thought. *This is a very bad dream.*

The other students stared at Albie for a while in silence. Scott was the first to speak. "Nice going, Albie. Now you've blown it for the rest of us."

"Yeah," said Brent, "and we were going to start memory work. You're a real jerk, Jensen. A dumb-ass idiot jerk."

"Leave him alone, Brent," said Cliff. "You don't care about memory work."

"But, Cliff . . ."

"Leave it, Brent."

"What happened to you, Albie?" Marla asked.

"You look terrible," said Leslie.

"Are you okay?" asked Maggie.

Albie didn't know what to say. There was nothing to say, really. "I'm . . . uh . . . sorry," he stammered. Then he turned and left the room.

"Albie!" shouted Mitch. "Wait!"

Albie waited outside the door. He was still drenched with sweat, but his breathing had slowed down. He was beginning to feel sick to his stomach. Mitch led him down the hall and around the corner. Then he stopped and examined him as if he were a scientific specimen. "You look like dogshit," he said.

Albie smiled slightly. "Thank you, Mitch. That's very kind."

"What did you do last night?"

Albie shrugged. "I don't know. I guess I had a couple more for the road."

Mitch whistled softly. "Albie Jensen. What am I gonna do with you?"

"Shoot me."

"You need some food. A nice fat juicy Chiefburger. Fries, milk shake—the works. I'll buy. Wait here and I'll get Maggie. Okay?"

"Uh, sure. My bike's in front. Why don't I wait for you there?"

"That's even better. See you in five—maybe ten. Maggie's in the john."

"Okay. See you there."

Mitch headed back toward Mr. Pierce's room. Albie

walked down the stairs and out the front door. As he bent over to unlock his bike, he could feel the insides of his stomach coming up his esophagus. The whiskey burned on the way down, but it burned even worse on the way up. He ran to the bushes along the side of the building, but he didn't make it. There was bologna, pizza, and whiskey all over the concrete. The bad dream was turning into a nightmare.

He took off his T-shirt and cleaned the puke off his face. Then he bent down and cleaned what he could off the sidewalk. When he was finished, he tossed the shirt into a trash can and walked back to his bike.

"Feeling better now?"

Albie looked toward the sound of the voice. Cliff Carlton was sitting in his Volkswagen convertible with the top down. He was leaning back in the driver's seat, watching Albie as if it were opening night at the opera. *Great. Not only do I puke all over the sidewalk, but I do it in front of Cliff.*

"Don't look so miserable," Cliff called. "C'mere a minute."

Albie rolled his bike over toward Cliff's car. When he got closer, he noticed that Cliff was wearing swim trunks. There was a towel and a cooler in the backseat.

"What you need," said Cliff, "is a day at the beach. Hop in."

"I've got my bike."

Cliff opened the driver's door and circled around the back of the car. "What do you think the bike rack's for? Roll that puppy over here."

He helped Cliff set his bike on the rack. When it

was in place, Cliff reached up and patted Albie on the cheek. "You're gonna live, buddy. As Pierce says, you *will* survive. Now let's get outta here."

Albie got into the passenger side as Cliff slipped behind the wheel. Cliff pressed his foot on the accelerator, and they pulled away from the school. "I'll take it easy," Cliff said. "If you feel sick, just do it over the side."

"I think I'm done."

"Good. There's some 7-Up and beer in the cooler. Help yourself. You're probably dehydrated."

Albie reached into the cooler and grabbed a 7-Up. It was ice cold. "You want something?" he asked.

"No, I'll wait."

Albie popped the top on the 7-Up and took a long drink. It felt good in his stomach. Very good.

"Beer's the best thing for a hangover," said Cliff.

"I think I'll stick to the 7-Up. Shit."

"What's wrong?"

"I just remembered something. I was supposed to meet Maggie and Mitch for lunch."

"You want me to turn around?"

"Naw, that's okay. They probably went ahead without me."

Cliff drove toward the lakefront in the wealthy part of town. Albie gazed at the houses along the way. Some were practically mansions, with wrought-iron gates and long, curving driveways.

"What a day!" said Cliff. "I usually go to the beach after the sessions. It's okay, but you don't get any rays."

"Thanks for taking me. You probably saved my life."

Cliff laughed. "Don't mention it. I hate to go alone."

"What happened to Brent and Stephanie?"

"Brent's a pain in the ass."

"What about Stephanie?"

"She's a pain, too, sometimes."

They were at the lakefront now. Cliff was slowly guiding the car down the street, looking for a parking place. Albie could feel the cool breeze blowing across his bare chest. The 7-Up had settled his stomach and rinsed the sour taste from his mouth. Things were looking up. He was actually going to the beach with Cliff Carlton.

Cliff carefully pulled the car into a space and hopped over the driver's door. He reached into the backseat for his towel. "Grab the cooler, would you?"

"Sure. What about my bike?"

Cliff thought for a moment. "Lock it to the bike rack. That'll be safe."

"Okay, sure." There was something about Cliff that made Albie feel everything was going to be all right. If Cliff said the bike was safe, then the bike was safe.

While Albie locked his bike, Cliff stood on the grass a few feet from the car. With his rolled towel tucked under his arm, he looked like a beachfront halfback, ready to break for the sand. "All set, big guy?"

"Yeah," said Albie, picking up the cooler. It seemed weird that Cliff would call him "big guy." Cliff had such a stocky, powerful build that he gave the impression of being a big guy himself. Actually Albie towered over him by six inches.

They walked across the grass toward the entrance to the beach. All the beaches in Wilmont were pretty much the same. There was a wide grassy strip along the street, with picnic benches, barbecue areas, and rest rooms. A fence of thin wooden slats separated the grass from the sand. You needed a token to get into the sand area, but it was pretty easy to hop the fence.

"Uh, Cliff, I'm gonna have to sneak around," said Albie. "I don't have my token."

Cliff glanced ahead at the entrance. There was a female lifeguard checking tokens. "Don't worry, buddy. I'll take care of it."

When they reached the gate, Cliff flashed his token at the girl. "Hi, Sharon. You're lookin' good."

The girl smiled. She was cute, but nothing special. Her shoulders were peeling, and there was a big white glob of zinc oxide on the end of her nose. "Hi, handsome. Where's Steph?"

"I left her home today. I brought my buddy instead. Albie, this is Sharon, the sexiest lifeguard on the beach."

Sharon laughed and tugged on the shoulder strap of her swimsuit. All the female lifeguards wore red one-piece suits that looked like they'd been washed four thousand times. "It's tough to be sexy in these things," she said.

"Not for you," said Cliff.

Sharon laughed again and shook her head. It was hard to tell under her dark suntan, but it looked like she was blushing. "Get in there," she said. "Nice to meet you, Albie."

"You, too."

With Albie bringing up the rear, Cliff walked through the gate and headed for an open spot on the sand. The beach was crowded with teenagers sunbathing, talking, listening to music, playing Frisbee, and just cruising the scene. There were more kids in the water, splashing around and tossing each other into the waves.

"This should do," said Cliff, spreading out his beach towel.

Albie set the cooler beside the towel and plopped down into the sand. "Yeow!" he yelped. "This sand is hot."

"Go ahead and sit on my towel," said Cliff. "There's room for both of us."

"Thanks." Albie sat on the edge of the towel and reached out to untie his shoelaces.

Cliff slipped his T-shirt over his head, kicked off his sandals, and sat down on the other side of the towel. "God, that sun feels good."

Albie stared for a moment at Cliff's chest. It was unbelievably hairy. He glanced down at his own. There was one miserable hair drooping down above his breastbone.

"Get me a beer, wouldya Albie? And stick it in that styrofoam thing."

Albie put a beer in the styrofoam container and handed it to Cliff. "Mind if I have another 7-Up?" he asked.

"Help yourself."

Albie took a long drink of the cold, fizzy soda. He closed his eyes and felt the hot sun soaking into his body. The air was fresh and the sounds of the beach were bright and easy. He was feeling better. He *would* survive. "This is great," he said.

Cliff smiled. "It's my beach."

Albie took another sip of 7-Up and dug his toes into the hot sand. "Mind if I ask you something?"

"Go ahead."

"Did you really mean that about Brent? Y'know—being a pain in the ass."

Cliff laughed and sipped his beer. "Definitely."

"So why are you friends?"

Cliff shrugged. "I've known him since we were kids."

"Oh."

"When I started acting, Brent thought it was really strange. Then all of a sudden he was trying out for plays and getting parts. He's no great actor, but he's pretty funny if he gets the right part."

"What about Stephanie?"

"What about her?"

"Do you really think she's a pain in the ass?"

Cliff took a sip of his beer and looked around the beach. "Over there," he said, "in the green."

Albie followed Cliff's gaze. There was a blond girl in a lime green bikini with curves that kept on curving.

"That's Stephanie," said Cliff.

"Huh?"

"All I have to do is walk over, give her the right line, and she's my Stephanie for today."

"Wow! Are you gonna do it?"

"Not now. Maybe later."

Cliff took another sip of beer. It was illegal to drink

on the beach, but he didn't seem concerned about it. "Look, Albie, Stephanie has a great body and she can be pretty sweet, but she isn't interesting. She's not an interesting person."

"Geez," said Albie. He didn't really know what to say. How could Stephanie not be interesting?

"Now take Pierce," Cliff continued, "he's just an old fag, but he's an amazing person. The guy knows more—"

"Wait a minute," said Albie. "What'd you say?"

"About what?"

"Mr. Pierce—what do you mean, he's an old fag?"

Cliff shrugged his shoulders. "He's gay. Everyone knows that."

Albie took a drink of his 7-Up. "Oh, of course. That kind of fag. Everyone knows that." *But if everyone knows it, how come I'm so surprised?*

"Anyway," Cliff continued, "that's not the point."

"What is the point?"

"The point is that Pierce is an extremely interesting person. He knows more about acting than the rest of the teachers combined. Not only that, he doesn't put up with any shit. Does he, Albert?" With the last question, Cliff slipped into a frightening imitation of Mr. Pierce's voice.

"Uh, no," said Albie. Suddenly the whole horrible scene in Mr. Pierce's room came back in full living color. "He's gonna kill me on Monday."

"He'll make you miserable."

Albie stared across the sand at the waves lapping gently against the shore. "What should I do?" he asked.

Cliff handed his empty can to Albie. "Apologize. On your knees."

Albie put the empty can in the cooler. "Do you want another beer?" he asked.

"Naw," said Cliff, gazing across the beach. "What I want is that girl in green."

ALBIE BOUNDED UP the back stairs two at a time. It had taken him the whole weekend to recover from the whiskey, but he felt like himself again. Maybe better than himself. The stairs seemed a little shorter, and the spring in his step was a little springier.

When he reached the top, he headed straight for Mr. Pierce's room. There was plenty of time, but he wanted to make sure he was early. As he approached the door, he noticed Cliff coming up the front stairs at the other end of the hall. Stephanie was beside him and Brent was a few steps behind. "Hurry up, buddy," Albie called. "You're gonna be late."

Cliff smiled and continued along at his steady pace. "You're lookin' a bit livelier there, big guy."

"I'm feeling livelier," said Albie. They were all four standing outside the door now.

"Did you have a nice time at the beach?" asked Stephanie. Her tone was friendly, but there was an edge to it. She didn't seem very happy.

Albie smiled broadly and looked at Cliff. "Yeah, it was great."

"C'mon," said Brent. "What are we standing around for?"

Cliff shook his head in exasperation. "Let's grab a seat before the poor guy explodes." He opened the door and, with his steady, driving stride, walked toward the plastic chairs in front of the stage. Albie and Stephanie followed on his heels, with Brent walking another step behind. The rest of the Company was already there, waiting for Mr. Pierce.

Out of habit, Albie began to walk toward his usual seat next to Mitch, but Cliff touched his arm lightly and ushered him into an empty seat at the end of the semi-circle. Cliff sat down beside him, and Stephanie sat beside Cliff. Brent seemed confused.

"Sit down, Brent," said Cliff. "What are you waiting for?" He turned toward Albie as if Brent had ceased to exist. "So, did you get some sleep?" he asked.

"Geez," said Albie, "I slept half the weekend."

"That's the way," said Cliff. "Stephanie wouldn't let me sleep at all."

"Why don't you broadcast it?" complained Stephanie.

"It's true," said Cliff.

"You don't have to tell half the world."

"Albie's not half the world."

"Yeah," said Albie, "I'm just a fourth of the world."

He noticed that Brent had gone to sit down next to Mitch. Mitch and Maggie were both looking at Albie strangely. *What do they want? I'm not required to sit next to them.*

At exactly 1:00, Mr. Pierce walked through the door and stepped to the front of the room. He looked slowly around the semicircle of students, as if to make sure that no one was missing. When he reached the last chair, his gaze lingered on Albie. The corners of his mouth turned up slightly into something between a smile and a sneer. *Here it comes*, Albie thought. One. Two. Three. Nothing. Mr. Pierce turned away and began the session.

"Memory is the essence of the Method. Relaxation and concentration are necessary in order to work on memory, but it is memory that leads to a believable and moving performance.

"Strasberg divided memory into two areas: sense memory and emotional memory. In sense memory work, the actor learns to reproduce the sensory experience of the real world. In emotional memory work, the actor learns to reproduce his own emotional experience."

"This sounds complicated," said Marla.

Mr. Pierce shook his head. "It isn't. Difficult, yes. But not complicated."

"What exactly do you mean by sensory experience?" asked Albie.

"Poor baby," said Stephanie. "You need a woman."

Everyone laughed at the joke. Albie could feel his face turning red.

"Very amusing, Stephanie," said Mr. Pierce. "Please bring your chair to the front."

Stephanie stood up and looked down at Cliff as

though she expected him to carry her chair. Cliff didn't move. Without thinking, Albie jumped to his feet, picked up the chair, and set it in the front of the room.

"Thank you, Albie," said Stephanie. "That's very sweet."

"Uh, sure." He sat down quickly. His face was still red.

"Her knight in shining armor," said Cliff. It was hard to tell if he was being friendly or sarcastic.

"All right, Stephanie," said Mr. Pierce. "Since you are an expert on sensory experience, I want you to feel the sun."

"Excuse me?"

"Sit in your chair and feel the sun shining on your face. Imagine you're on the beach or sitting in a park."

"Am I wearing a bathing suit?"

"Spare me," said Maggie.

"If you wish," said Mr. Pierce. "But for this exercise, I want you to concentrate on your face. Are you ready?"

"I guess so."

"Begin."

Stephanie turned her face up toward an imaginary sun. She closed her eyes and wrinkled the end of her nose. She raised her eyebrows and stretched the skin on her forehead. Then she stretched her arms out lazily to the sides. Albie stared at her breasts underneath her tight T-shirt. *Cliff must be crazy. With a body like that, who needs interesting?*

After a minute or so, Mr. Pierce stopped the exercise. "Thank you, Stephanie. Any comments?"

"It was great," said Albie.

Mr. Pierce fixed Albie with his cold sneer-smile. "Any intelligent comments?" he asked.

"She did everything too fast," said Marla.

"I thought she was trying to smell the sun," said Maggie.

"It was good," said Scott. "The way she stretched her skin was very believable."

"Anything else?" asked Mr. Pierce. "Remember— this is an exercise in sense memory. What was missing?"

The room was silent as the students considered the question. After a few moments, there was a quiet, hesitant response.

"Heat."

Albie looked around the semicircle to see who had spoken. It was Jennifer DiPino. He was amazed. In two weeks, she had never volunteered a word.

Mr. Pierce seemed equally surprised. "Speak up, Jennifer. We can't hear you."

Jennifer's olive complexion turned a shade darker. "I said heat," she repeated, slightly louder than before. "There was no sense of heat. She seemed to be reacting mostly to the light."

Mr. Pierce smiled. "Excellent, Jennifer. Excellent. Stephanie's performance gave no indication of temperature. Her sun might have been cold or hot or somewhere in between."

"How am I supposed to show the difference?" asked Stephanie.

"You don't *show* anything," said Mr. Pierce. "You remember the actual sensation of the sun's warmth and you reproduce it on the stage."

"But I *was* remembering it."

"You thought you were remembering," said Mr. Pierce, "but true sense memory only comes through practice. I want each of you to choose a simple, everyday experience—sitting in the sun, making a breakfast drink, taking a shower. Repeat that experience every day for the next three days. Observe everything—the way it tastes and smells and sounds and feels. On Thursday, we'll each do our experience for the group."

"Mr. Pierce?"

"Yes, Scott?"

"It seems like this is just pantomime. I mean, in most plays you've got props and lights and everything to help you create a reality."

Mr. Pierce nodded. "That's true. But remember, no matter how many props we have on the stage, theater is make-believe. The actor must make the audience believe that he is someone he is not, that he is doing things he is not doing, that he exists in a place he does not exist. It is only through developing our sense memory that we can create that kind of reality.

"I'll give you an example. In *King Lear*, there's a famous scene where Lear stands in a great storm and bellows, 'Blow, winds, crack your cheeks! rage! blow!' " Mr. Pierce bellowed the words across the room. Then he continued in his normal voice.

"Now, I've seen many Lears. Some had deep, strong voices. Others were stately old men, physically suited to the part. But the best was a young fellow from the Actors Studio—not much older than some of you." He looked at the students as though he were searching for the young actor. His eyes rested on Cliff, and a smile spread slowly outward from the corners of his mouth. "He was the only Lear who made me feel the wind."

When the session was over, Albie pretended that he was looking for something under his chair. Actually, there was nothing under his chair except the linoleum, but he didn't want to make it obvious that he was waiting around.

"What are you doing, Albert?" asked Mr. Pierce. "It's time to lock up." He stood above Albie, his huge ring of keys in his hand. His face and voice were expressionless. It was obvious he was still angry.

"Uh, yes, sir. I just . . . well, I wanted to say I was sorry for being late on Friday."

Mr. Pierce continued to eye him coldly. "Do you like school, Albert?"

Albie had to think for a moment. It wasn't that he had any doubts—he just wasn't expecting the question. "Uh, yeah . . . sure, I like school."

"What's your favorite subject?"

"Drama." He didn't have to think about that one.

"Other than drama."

Albie shifted in his chair. "Math, I guess."

"Are you good at mathematics?"

"Yes, sir. Straight A's."

Mr. Pierce twirled his key ring in his hand. "Excellent," he said. "I suggest you become an accountant. Because you will never be an actor." He walked toward the back of the room and switched off the lights.

Albie rose from his plastic chair and turned to go. He could see Mr. Pierce's tall, thin silhouette outlined in the doorway. The only sound was the jangling of the key ring. As Albie crossed the room, he felt anger surging within him. *Is it true you're an old faggot?* he said. Only he didn't say it. He would never say it. Instead he stopped in the doorway and looked Mr. Pierce directly in the eyes.

"I want to be an actor."

Mr. Pierce stopped playing with the key ring. Although his mouth was as expressionless as before, there was the hint of a smile in his eyes.

"Show me."

Albie stood for a moment with him in the doorway. Then he left the room and descended the back stairs. When he reached the first floor, he opened the back door and exited into the hot, humid afternoon. Mitch and Maggie were waiting in front of the trees near his special place. He wasn't surprised to see them.

"Hi," he said, trying to crack a smile. "Wanta go to Burger Chief?"

Mitch took a long drag on his cigarette. "Where were you?" he asked.

"Talking to Pierce."

"I mean on Friday."

Albie glanced at the empty playing field. "Oh, that. I got sick and Cliff drove me home."

"Uh-huh."

"We were really worried about you," said Maggie. The sun was shining on her face. He couldn't really see her eyes, but her skin was glowing.

"Yeah . . . I'm sorry."

Mitch took another drag on his cigarette. "Your bike

was missing, so we figured you got it wrong—that you were gonna meet us there. We walked over and waited about forty minutes. Then we came back and looked for you here. Then we called your house. No one was home."

"Uh, yeah . . . I put a pillow over the phone."

"Right. C'mon, Maggie, let's get out of here." Mitch grabbed Maggie by the arm and they began to walk away. After a few steps, Mitch turned and called back to Albie. "The part's the same."

"What are you talking about?"

"We saw you following Cliff into class."

"So what?"

"So it doesn't matter whether it's Brent or you— it's still the Fool."

"Screw you," said Albie.

Mitch took Maggie's hand and walked away.

"THEY STINK!" Albie shouted. "I can't believe these guys!" The Sox were down 7–3 in the bottom of the ninth. They were heading for three losses in a row. "When's dinner ready?" he called. "I'm starving."

"Dinner's ready when I say it's ready."

His mother had been a little testy since the whiskey business. Things were looking up though. She was making his favorite meal—meatballs with rice and tomato sauce.

There were two outs and no one on when the telephone rang in the kitchen. His mother poked her head into the living room. "It's for you," she said.

Albie looked up in surprise. "Who is it?"

Mrs. Jensen frowned impatiently. "Get the phone, Albie. I'm in the middle of dinner."

Albie jumped to his feet. The telephone was on the

wall above the kitchen counter. He picked up the receiver and stepped out of his mother's way.

"Hello," he said. "Yeah . . . Oh, hi . . . Really? . . . Yeah, I think so. Of course, I'll have to check my calendar. . . . Sure, no problem . . . Great . . . No problem at all . . . Uh-huh . . . Uh, thanks, Brent. 'Bye."

Albie hung up the phone and glanced into the living room. The game was over.

"What was that all about?" his mother asked. She was in the middle of flipping the meatballs.

"Brent Matthews invited me to a party."

"Who's Brent Matthews?"

"He's in the Company."

"Does he drink whiskey?"

"Geez, Mom, I don't know."

"When is it?"

"This Saturday night. Can I go?"

Mrs. Jensen turned away from the stove and eyed him warily. "No drinking."

"No drinking. Absolutely."

"Where is it?"

"His house. It's one of those big places down by the lake. Brent's pretty rich."

Mrs. Jensen went back to the meatballs. "How are you getting there?"

Albie drummed his fingertips on the countertop and watched his mother's back. "I thought maybe I could borrow the car."

"Absolutely not."

"Aw, c'mon, Mom. I'm a great driver."

Mrs. Jensen picked up the wooden spoon and stirred

the tomato sauce. "I don't care if you're Mario Andretti," she said, speaking into the sauce. "You're not driving until you have a driver's license. Period."

"I have a learner's permit."

"Period." She was still talking to the sauce.

"Please?"

She lifted the spoon out of the sauce, turned around, and pointed it at him. "Period," she repeated. Albie watched as the sauce dripped off the spoon and onto the kitchen floor. That was it. Three periods and tomato sauce on the floor.

"Uh, yeah. Okay, I understand. I'll just clean this up." He grabbed a paper towel and wiped up the tomato sauce. "Boy, that sure smells good."

"Turn off the TV and set the table. We'll be ready in a minute."

"Sure."

When the table was set, Mrs. Jensen dished out the meatballs and rice and poured the tomato sauce on top. Albie dug in with enthusiasm. "This is great, Mom. Absolutely great. Just terrific."

His mother smiled. "Maybe Mitch can drive you," she said.

"Uh, no," said Albie. "I don't think so."

"Why not?"

"We had a little argument. Besides, I don't think he's invited."

Mrs. Jensen looked up from her food. "What do you mean he's not invited? He's in the Company."

"Yeah, but I don't think this is a Company party. I mean Brent's got lots of different friends. Anyway, he told me to keep it to myself."

"I see."

Albie and his mother ate awhile in silence. Finally, Mrs. Jensen looked up and said, "I guess I'll have to take you."

"I thought you were going out with Roger."

"We'll work around it. I think this is important for you."

Albie played with his food. He liked to see if he could pick up every grain of rice with his fork. "Geez, Mom. I really appreciate the sacrifice and everything, but I don't know. It's kind of weird."

"What's so weird? I drop you off and pick you up."

"Yeah, but what about my date?"

"Your date? What date?"

Albie looked at her in exasperation. She tried so hard, but sometimes she didn't know anything. "I have to get a date. It's couples only."

Mrs. Jensen leaned over the table in excitement. "Who's the lucky girl?"

Albie looked down at his plate. There were three grains of rice left, but no matter how hard he tried there was no way he could pick them up with his fork. "Beats me."

Albie locked his bicycle in the secret spot and walked toward the back door of the school. Since Brent's phone call, he'd been thinking about who he would ask to the party. He'd never really had a date. Of course a party wasn't exactly a regular date, but it was pretty close. Anyway, he had to ask somebody and she had to say yes. That's what it came down to.

As he thought about the girls he knew, he kept

coming up with Stephanie and Maggie. Why did he have this thing for his friends' girlfriends? It was self-destructive. What he needed was a girl for *him*.

The more he thought about it, the more he decided that the only answer was Jennifer. She had a pretty face and a cute body. She was no dummy, either. But the main thing was that she seemed to like him. She always smiled at him. Wasn't that what girls did when they liked someone? How should he know? Anyway, Jennifer was the one. She had to be.

At the top of the stairs, Albie noticed Brent coming out of the bathroom and walking toward Mr. Pierce's room. He picked up his own pace and tried to catch him. "Hey, Brent!" he called. "Wait up."

Brent turned around and waited impatiently. "Yeah?"

Albie caught up to him and smiled. "I just wanted to say thanks again. You know—for inviting me to the party."

Brent shrugged his shoulders. "Cliff made me do it. He thinks you have potential."

Albie squinted down at Brent as if he were talking nonsense. "Potential? What kind of potential?"

"How should I know? I didn't say it."

"Oh. Well, geez, uh, thanks anyway. I mean for the invitation."

"Yeah, sure. You got a date yet? It's couples only, remember." Brent's tone was an obvious challenge.

"Of course I have a date. I'm bringing Jennifer." As soon as the words were out, Albie knew he was in trouble.

"Jennifer? From the class?"

Albie stood up to his full height. He was in it now. "Yeah. Anything wrong with that?"

"No, that's fine. Just tell her not to spread it around. I can only stand so many drama people at one time. Y'know what I mean?"

"Yeah, sure. I feel the same way."

Brent turned around and headed for Mr. Pierce's room. Albie caught up to him in a few steps. "Listen, Brent," he said, "if you'd like your old seat back, I mean it doesn't really matter to me."

Brent stopped and looked up at Albie. "Save it, Jensen."

Albie followed Brent into the room. Cliff and Stephanie were sitting in their usual places. Brent sat down next to Stephanie, and Albie sat next to Cliff.

"Hey, big guy," said Cliff. "Got your date lined up for the big bash?"

"Sure. I'm taking Jennifer."

"Great."

"She's cute," said Stephanie.

"Yeah," said Albie. *Great, she's cute, except I haven't asked her yet.* He kept his eye on the door. Marla and Leslie came in, followed by Mitch and Maggie. Mitch ignored him, but Maggie gave him a nice smile.

Albie glanced at his watch. It was five minutes until one. If he did it fast, he might catch Jennifer on her way into class. He turned to Cliff. "I have to go to the bathroom."

Cliff laughed. "Well, go."

"Uh, yeah, right." Albie got up and went out into

the hall. He waited casually halfway between the bathroom and the door. Mr. Pierce walked past him a minute later. "Almost time, Albert," he said.

"Yes, sir. I have to go to the bathroom."

"Make it fast."

Albie could feel his heart beating hard in his chest. Where the heck was she? Suddenly Jennifer appeared at the top of the front stairway. This was it. The moment of truth. He walked toward her as if he were coming out of the bathroom. Then he noticed that she was with Scott. They were walking quickly, chatting away like old buddies.

Albie stopped in his tracks and pretended that he had dropped something on the floor. He could see Jennifer and Scott's feet passing him by. "Hurry up, Albie," Jennifer called. "It's almost time."

He turned around and followed them into the room like a walking zombie. *This is not right. What if she's got a date with Scott? This is definitely not right.* He was still a zombie when he sat down next to Cliff and Mr. Pierce began the session. *What do I do now? I told everyone I'm taking Jennifer. I'm gonna look like a total jerk. Maybe that's my potential. Maybe it's all some kind of plot to bring out my total-jerk potential. Maybe I'm beyond potential. Maybe I already am a total jerk. Maybe . . .*

"Albert. We are waiting."

Albie snapped out of zombiehood to find Mr. Pierce staring down at him. "Oh, yes, of course. Sorry. I'm ready. Completely ready." *Ready for what?* He was so disoriented, he couldn't remember what they were supposed to do. As he stood up, he glanced toward Cliff.

Cliff casually lifted his hand to his face as if he were scratching the stubble on his cheek. When his mouth was hidden from Mr. Pierce, he silently mouthed the word: "Experience."

Albie stepped to the front of the room. *Whew! Thank you, Cliff.* He'd been practicing his experience for three days, but it didn't seem very important right now. "Experience," he mumbled. "Experience, experience, experi—"

"Did you say something, Albert?"

"I was just getting into character."

"We are waiting."

Albie took a deep breath, closed his eyes, and tried to concentrate. When he was ready, he began to unbutton his shirt. Actually, he pretended to unbutton his shirt, his fingers moving a few millimeters above the real buttons. He pulled his arms out of the sleeves, took the shirt off, and dropped it on the floor. Then he took off his pants, underpants, socks, and shoes. When he was completely naked, he stepped toward an imaginary bathtub, leaned over, and turned on the water—first the hot, then the cold. He tested the water rushing out of the spout and adjusted the handles to get it just right. Then he pulled the shower valve and stepped into the tub.

The water felt like tiny warm needles playing softly against his skin. He turned his face up toward the shower head, closed his eyes, and recoiled slightly as the spray pounded against his face. He reached for the shampoo, poured a little into the palm of his left hand, and dripped it onto the top of his head. He set the bottle down and worked the shampoo into his hair with both hands. Then he bent forward toward the shower head and rinsed his hair.

Next, he picked up a bar of soap and played it between his palms, working up a thick lather. He washed his neck and shoulders, lathered again, and moved on to his chest and arms, his stomach and genitalia, his lower back and buttocks, and finally his long legs. He was constantly aware of the slipperiness of his soapy hand against his skin. Finally, he washed his face, wincing as the soap stung his eyes. He rinsed off, feeling the warm soothing wetness against his body. Then he turned off the water, stepped out of the shower, and began to dry himself. The towel felt rough and good against the open pores of his skin. He rubbed his head vigorously. Then he set the towel over a bar and looked up at Mr. Pierce.

"Comments?" asked Mr. Pierce.

"I thought it was good," said Scott. "He had most of the details."

"He's still naked," said Cliff.

"I like that," murmured Stephanie.

Standing in the front of the room, Albie could feel himself blushing. It was ridiculous. He was fully dressed, but he actually felt naked.

"The details were fine," said Mr. Pierce. "And there was no need to get dressed. In fact, there was no need to get undressed. The point of the exercise is the sensual experience of the shower."

"There was a real sense of heat," offered Maggie. "I could almost feel the steam."

"He washed his hair too quickly," said Marla, "but he did a great job on the body."

"Testing the water was very believable," added Leslie.

"It was wonderful," said Jennifer. "Everything. The heat of the water, the wetness, the slipperiness of the soap, even the towel."

"Thanks," said Albie. "I really worked on it."

"Albert," Mr. Pierce admonished, "may I remind you that the actor is not to respond until the critique is finished."

"Oh, yeah. Sure. Sorry."

"Anything else?" Mr. Pierce waited for a moment. Albie glanced toward Mitch, but Mitch wouldn't meet his eyes. *Screw you again*, he thought.

"Well, Albert," said Mr. Pierce, "I agree with the class that you did a fine job. There is always more that an actor can do, but I think that for our level at this particular time you have re-created your experience as well as can be expected. You may rejoin the group."

As Albie returned to his seat, Cliff gave him a pat on the shoulder and whispered, "You look good naked." Albie smiled. Maybe now Mr. Pierce would understand that he was a serious actor. And Jennifer definitely liked him. There was no doubt about it.

When the session was over, Albie followed Jennifer out of the room. She was still walking next to Scott, but it wasn't like they were boyfriend and girlfriend or anything. At least he hoped they weren't. When they started walking down the long hallway toward the front stairs, he followed at a discreet distance, pretending to look for something in a couple of lockers along the way. He continued down the stairs, lagging a flight behind. He could hear them clearly, talking and laughing away.

On the main floor, he looked into a few more lockers as Jennifer and Scott took their time around the front door. Most of the lockers were empty, but in one he found an old peanut butter sandwich and a pair of underpants. *Great. First I'm investigating the mystery of life. Now I'm investigating lockers.* Finally, Scott and Jennifer left the building. Albie lurked in the doorway as they talked near the bike racks in front of the school. *C'mon, Scott, say good-bye, say good-bye, good-bye, Jennifer, see you tomorrow, good-bye.*

Out on the sidewalk, Scott finally said good-bye and started to walk north. Jennifer walked south. Albie waited until Scott was out of sight. Then he loped down the outside stairs and followed Jennifer. She was already halfway up the hill to the railroad tracks, but he caught up quickly. He was a slow runner, but he was one heck of a walker.

"Jennifer! Wait a minute."

Jennifer turned around. "Albie! I didn't even know you were there."

"Yeah, well, I saw you walking along, and I'm going the same way, so I just thought I'd catch up and walk with you. If you don't mind."

"No, of course not. I didn't know you walked this way."

"Well, actually I rode my bike, but you know I was just wondering—there's this party this weekend, and I was wondering if you'd like to go with me." It wasn't exactly smooth, but at least he got it out.

Jennifer looked up at him. She wasn't short, but he still towered over her. "I'd love to," she said.

"Of course I understand if you can't, but I was hoping that maybe you could. It's a great party. Down by the lake. A fancy house. You know . . ."

"Albie, I said I'd love to."

Albie looked down at her in amazement. "Oh. Great. I mean that's really great."

Jennifer smiled sweetly. "I think so, too."

"How do I look?" asked Albie. He was wearing his best jeans, a print shirt, and a brand-new pair of glorified gym shoes.

Mrs. Jensen reached over to brush a stray hair from his forehead. They were sitting in the car outside of Jennifer's house. "You look beautiful," she said. "I mean handsome. Devastatingly handsome."

"You always say that."

"I say it because it's true. Now go and get Jennifer."

Albie opened the passenger door and walked up the sidewalk to Jennifer's house. It was a few blocks from their apartment—nothing fancy, but bigger than he had expected. As he rang the doorbell, he felt his heart pounding in his chest. This was his first date. *What are you supposed to do on a date, anyway?*

Jennifer's father opened the door. He was a handsome, dark-haired man, wearing a sport coat and slacks. Albie stared at him stupidly.

"You must be Albie," said Mr. DiPino.

"Yes, sir," Albie stammered. "I must be. I mean, I am."

Mr. DiPino smiled. "Come in. Jennifer will be out in a minute."

As Albie walked into the house, he glanced back toward the car.

"Is someone waiting for you?" Mr. DiPino asked.

"Uh, yes. My mother. She's driving us."

"How nice of her. Why don't you ask her in?"

"Oh, no. I mean, thank you very much, but we're kind of in a hurry." That's all he needed—his mother drinking coffee with the DiPinos while he and Jennifer sat there like a couple of idiots.

Mr. DiPino nodded pleasantly. "I understand. We're on our way out ourselves." He glanced at his watch and called toward the back of the house. "Jennifer, Albie's here. Dolores, we're running late."

Two female voices responded like an echo. "Almost ready." "Almost ready."

Mr. DiPino smiled knowingly. "Women. Give 'em a minute and they take an hour."

Albie nodded in agreement. "Absolutely, sir. I say that all the time."

A minute later, Jennifer entered the living room. She was wearing a pair of stone-washed jeans and a white blouse.

"Hi, Albie."

"Hi, Jennifer."

"Well," said Mr. DiPino, "I'd better hurry my wife. You kids have a nice time. Jennifer, I want you home by eleven." He turned away from Jennifer and stared directly into Albie's eyes. His face was still pleasant, but his eyes were intense—deep dark brown with pupils like black holes. "I'm holding you responsible," he said.

"Uh, no problem, sir. My mother's coming to pick us up."

"Good. Have fun, honey. You look beautiful." Mr. DiPino bent down and kissed Jennifer on the forehead.

"Good night, Dad," said Jennifer.

As Albie watched Mr. DiPino disappear down the hall, he started to get nervous again. Part of it was about being on a date, but part of it was about Mr. DiPino. He seemed like a pretty nice guy, but those eyes were scary.

"Albie?"

"Huh?"

"Are you ready to go?"

"Oh, yeah, sure. I was just thinking."

Jennifer smiled. "You look very nice," she said.

Albie could feel himself turning red. "Oh, thanks. So do you."

They walked out the front door and down the sidewalk toward the car. The sun had set, but the heat of the day still lingered in the air. Albie opened the rear door and let Jennifer into the backseat. Then he opened the front door and got in beside his mother.

"Hi, Mom. Sorry we took so long."

His mother looked at him like he was totally insane. "Albie, don't you think you should sit with Jennifer?"

Albie glanced at Jennifer and then looked back at his mother. "Oh, yeah. Of course. Sorry." He opened the front door, climbed out, closed the front door, opened the rear door, and climbed into the backseat beside Jennifer.

"Sorry," he repeated. "I wasn't thinking right. I mean, we only have two seats in the front and, you know, I always . . ."

"That's okay, Albie," said Jennifer. "Hello, Mrs. Jensen. I'm Jennifer DiPino."

Mrs. Jensen turned around and smiled warmly. "Hello, Jennifer. Very nice to meet you."

In the backseat, Albie untied one of his size twelve glorified gym shoes and pounded himself on the head. Actually he didn't, but he wanted to. It was ten minutes into his first date, and he already looked like a total doofus.

As they rode toward the party, Albie tried to think of something interesting to say. It was weird. He had no trouble talking to Jennifer at the sessions. But they weren't at the sessions. They were on a date.

"Uh, it's pretty hot," he said finally.

Jennifer smiled at him like he was the Albert Einstein of meteorology. "Yeah," she replied, "really hot."

"This is the address," said Mrs. Jensen. "The house must be up the driveway." She pulled off the main road and onto a gravel driveway lined with tall elm trees. They couldn't see the house yet, but there were flashes of light between the trees.

"Wow!" Albie exclaimed. "This is some driveway."

"It's really pretty," said Jennifer.

"Most of these houses are set back on the lake," said Mrs. Jensen.

"Wow!" said Albie. "That's some house." It was a mock-Tudor mansion with windows and windows and more windows. Bright lights illuminated the grounds and rock music blared into the night. Cars were crammed into the end of the driveway and scattered on the lawn. "Geez, it's like *The Great Gatsby* or something."

"I'll just let you kids off here," said Mrs. Jensen, pulling over to the side of the driveway.

"Sure, Mom. This is fine." Albie opened the door and climbed out of the backseat. He was about to close the door behind him when he remembered to hold it open for Jennifer.

"Thanks for driving us, Mrs. Jensen," said Jennifer as she slid out of the backseat.

"My pleasure. Now, I'll meet you right here at quarter to eleven."

"Great," said Albie, leaning through the open door, "quarter 'til."

"Do you have your watch?"

"I'm sure they have clocks. Thanks, Mom." Albie closed the door and stood beside Jennifer as Mrs. Jensen turned the car around and headed back down the driveway. The night was still hot, but there was a slight breeze blowing off the lake.

"Your mother's really nice," said Jennifer.

Albie shrugged. "She's okay. I mean, I could have driven, but I won't actually have my license until the end of the month. It's just a technicality."

Jennifer smiled and waited as if she expected him

to say something else. It was the first time they were actually alone on their date.

"Well, uh, I guess we better go inside now."

"Sure."

As they walked toward the house, Albie glanced down nervously at Jennifer. It was amazing—she just gave him that sweet little waiting-for-something smile. *What's she waiting for? What am I supposed to do? Kiss her? Hold her hand? Say something brilliant?*

When they reached the door, Albie pressed the doorbell and waited. The music was so loud that he couldn't tell if the bell was working or not. "Maybe we should just go in," he shouted over the music.

Jennifer smiled and said, "I don't know." At least that's what Albie thought she said. Her voice was so soft that he could barely hear her.

Albie pressed the doorbell again and waited for another minute. Then he turned the knob and slowly opened the door. It was kind of weird walking into someone's house but, after all, he'd been invited. There was nobody in the front hallway. "It sounds like the music's coming from the back," he yelled.

At the end of the hallway, there was a spiral staircase leading to the second floor. To the right of the staircase was a huge living room with three couches and a grand piano. There were two people making out pretty heavily on one of the couches. Albie glanced at Jennifer. She was still smiling, but she looked kind of nervous. He nodded toward the back of the house, and they continued walking toward the music.

They passed through another living room and a formal dining room with a table that looked like something out of King Arthur. Then they walked through a kitchen that was practically as big as his whole apartment. There were two refrigerators, three ovens, and enough counter space to slice most of the vegetables in Wilmont.

Finally, they ended up in a huge room with three plate-glass windows overlooking the lake. The music was so loud that the windows were shaking. There were about thirty people dancing in the middle of the room and thirty more just hanging out around the sides. Opposite the windows, there was a disc jockey playing records and tapes through huge speakers. On the far wall, a bartender in a tuxedo was mixing drinks. Next to the bartender was a table full of cold cuts and hors d'oeuvres. *Geez . . .*

Albie looked around the room for someone he knew. He recognized some people from school, but they weren't kids he talked to. More precisely, they were kids who didn't talk to him. Brent was over by the deejay, yelling into his ear. Albie walked toward him, and Jennifer followed. When it looked like Brent was finished with the deejay, Albie tapped him on the shoulder. Brent turned around and flashed a maniacal smile.

"Hey, Jensen!" he screamed. "Welcome to my nightmare!"

Albie stared at him. He'd known Brent for two years, but he'd never seen him like this. He was a completely different person. His cheeks were flushed with color, and his eyes were glowing. He was a party animal.

"Nice house," Albie yelled.

Brent looked down at Jennifer and cased her from head to foot as if he could see right through her clothes.

"Jennifer! You look hot—and I don't mean the weather!"

Jennifer smiled uncomfortably and looked up at Albie.

Brent reached into the back pocket of his jeans, pulled out a small silver flask, and offered it to Albie. "Want a drink?" he asked.

"What's in it?"

"One-fifty-one. My private stash."

Albie shook his head. "No. Thanks anyway."

Brent unscrewed the top of the flask and took a long swallow. Then he screwed the top on and wiped his lips with the back of his hand. "Wow!" he yelled. "Awhoooooo!"

When Brent stopped howling, Albie bent closer to his ear and asked, "Where are Cliff and Stephanie?"

Brent shrugged. "Look in the bedrooms . . . Awhooooo!"

Albie watched as Brent danced away and disappeared into the crowd at the center of the room. *The werewolf of Wilmont.* He looked down at Jennifer to see how she was handling it. She gave him the smile.

"Wanna dance?" he yelled.

"Sure," she screamed.

Albie walked toward the middle of the room, and Jennifer followed a step behind. When he found a spot that seemed like it was in the official dance area, he turned around and started moving in time to the music. At least, he hoped it was in time to the music. He wasn't much of a dancer. No matter how cool he tried to be, his size twelve glorified gym shoes had other plans. Jennifer was pretty good. She could really move her feet and hips and swing her arms with the rhythm.

When the song was over, Albie motioned toward the bartender and yelled, "Wanna get something to drink?" He couldn't believe how loud his voice sounded. Then he realized that the music had stopped. People were staring at him. Albie looked down at the floor and walked toward the bartender.

"That was fun," said Jennifer.

"Yeah. Geez, I'm thirsty." His shirt was drenched with sweat. But everybody else was sweaty, too. Even Jennifer.

On the bartender's table there were bottles of whiskey, scotch, gin, vodka, tequila, and wine. Behind the table was a big barrel full of ice and bottles of imported beer.

"What can I get for you, sir?" asked the bartender.

Albie eyed the cold beer. It looked good, especially after dancing. But he'd promised his mother to stay sober. "Do you have any 7-Up?" he asked.

"Yes, sir. And for the lady?"

"Diet Coke," said Jennifer.

"Coming right up."

When they had their drinks, they walked over toward the windows and looked out at the lake. There were floodlights shining on the sand, and they could see the waves lapping at the shore. After a few moments the music started up again, but Albie was so fascinated by the view from the window that he didn't pay much attention. Suddenly he felt a tap on his shoulder. He turned around and his jaw nearly dropped to his shoes. It was Stephanie, and she was dressed to thrill. Or kill.

Or something. She was wearing high heels, a short, tight skirt, and a blouse that looked a size too small. Stephanie always looked great, but this was a new definition of greatness. The jayster agreed completely.

"Wanna dance?" she asked.

"Sure." He was already walking toward the dance floor when he remembered Jennifer. "Do you mind?"

Jennifer smiled, but it wasn't exactly sweet. "Have fun," she said.

Stephanie grabbed his hand and pulled him into the crowd of people. When they found a space, she turned around and started moving with the music. Stephanie could dance. The way she moved her hips made Jennifer look like a mannequin. Not to mention the way her breasts moved under that tight blouse. At first, Albie just stared at her. Then he started shuffling his big feet around to distract the jayster. It didn't work.

When the song was over, Stephanie looked up at him with a sexy smile and said, "That was great. Let's do it some more."

The next song was already starting. "Where's Cliff?" Albie asked.

"How should I know?" she yelled over the music. "We're not Siamese twins." She stepped back and began gyrating to the beat. Albie did his best to follow along, but it was hopeless. Stephanie didn't seem to mind.

During the third song, Albie looked around the room for Jennifer. She was over by the bartender's table, talking to some big football player. He was about 6'5" and had a neck like a baby oak tree. *If that's her type, it's fine with me.* He looked back at Stephanie. It seemed like she was getting sexier with every dance—if that was possible. *This is my type*, he thought.

In the middle of the next dance, Stephanie stepped closer and wrapped her arms around his neck. She pulled him down toward her and whispered into his ear, "I'm hot. Let's get out of here."

Albie nodded and followed her off the dance floor. They walked back out through the kitchen, the dining room, and the two living rooms. The same couple was still making out on the couch in the front living room. They hadn't even changed position. Stephanie grabbed Albie's hand.

"C'mon," she said. "Let's go outside."

The night was still hot. Even with the breeze from the lake, the air was thick and humid. "These kind of nights make me crazy," Albie said.

"Yeah?" said Stephanie. "I like crazy men."

She led him around the house and down a narrow path toward the lake. The beach lay directly in front of them, lit by the floodlights. Albie had a vision of making out with Stephanie on the sand, in full view of the entire party. That would be a night to remember.

"Over here," she said.

He followed her off the path and away from the house. After a few yards, the beach narrowed to a thin strip. On the right, the sand rose abruptly to the tall elm trees of the Matthews' grounds. On the left, giant boulders kept the lake from washing over the beach.

Stephanie stopped and turned toward him. She wrapped her arms around his neck and lifted her face up toward his. He could smell her perfume and feel her breasts pressing against the front of his shirt. He didn't stop to think. It just happened. His lips were touching hers and electricity was exploding in his brain.

Oh my God! This is it. This is what it's all about.

After a few minutes, they broke apart for air. Albie was breathing heavily. Stephanie pressed her body against his and ran her tongue along the side of his neck. "Did you like that?" she whispered.

"Yeah," Albie panted. He looked around for some-place more comfortable. "Let's go into the trees."

"No, the rocks." She took his hand and led him over to the boulders. He could see the spray of the waves as they crashed against the other side, but the rocks along the sand were dry. Stephanie found a broad, flat slab of granite and leaned back against it. "Lift me up," she said.

Albie put his hands tentatively around her waist. He was still breathing hard. His heart was beating like a jackhammer.

"What are you waiting for?"

"Nothing." He lifted her onto the rock and pulled himself up beside her. Without another word, they were back in each other's arms. He wrapped his right hand around the back of her skirt and pulled her onto his lap. With his left hand, he reached slowly toward her breasts. *Will she let me? Will she? Will she? Yes!* He massaged her breasts through her blouse. They were big and round and soft and firm all at the same time.

Albie inched his hand toward the buttons of her blouse. He tried to undo the button between her breasts, but he couldn't get it. After a few fumbles, Stephanie lifted her own hand and undid it for him. Then she took his hand and placed it against her bra, showing him how she wanted to be touched.

He could feel a light spray coming over the rocks from the lake. The waves were getting bigger, but he wasn't moving. He was never moving. Casually, he dropped his left hand and let it fall to Stephanie's thigh. He brushed his fingers softly back and forth against her stockings. Then, very slowly, he inched his way toward the opening in her skirt. *This is heaven. This is ecstasy. I am going to touch it. I am going to touch it. I am going to touch it.* Just as his hand slipped under the hem of her skirt, Stephanie pulled it away with the quick moves of an expert.

"I think we better go back inside."

Albie was panting like he'd run the bases fourteen times. "Why?" he asked.

"It's late."

"So?"

Stephanie smiled pleasantly as she buttoned up her blouse. "So you might turn into a pumpkin."

They walked back toward the house arm in arm. The jayster was in so much pain that Albie could barely walk in a straight line. *Geez, how can so much pleasure cause so much pain?* As they walked into the house, Stephanie broke away from him. "What's wrong?" he asked.

"Trust me."

"Okay."

At the end of the hall, they ran into Cliff coming down the spiral staircase with a knockout blonde. She was wearing tight jeans and a halter top that barely covered her breasts. Albie had a feeling he'd seen her before. Then he remembered. It was the girl in green from the beach.

"Hello, Albie," said Cliff. "Enjoying the party?"

"Uh, yeah. It's great. Nice house."

Stephanie took Albie's arm and looked directly at Cliff, totally ignoring the girl in green. "Yes," she said. "Albie and I have been having a wonderful time."

"I'm sure you have," said Cliff. "We were just going to grab a drink. Care to join us?"

"We'd love to," said Stephanie. "I'm sooo thirsty."

When they reached the party room, Brent was in the center of the dance floor, spinning in circles and howling away. "Awhoooooo! Awhoooooo!" The rest of the people were watching from the sidelines, laughing and egging him on. Albie scanned the room for Jennifer. He spotted the big football jock, passed out with a bottle of tequila in his hand, but Jennifer wasn't with him. His eyes were closed, and there was drool running down his chin. The guy was history. The only other person who would know Jennifer was Brent, but he was too busy howling.

"What time is it?" Albie asked Stephanie, but it was Cliff who answered.

"Eleven. Brent howls on the hour."

"Shit! Listen, Stephanie, I really have to go."

Stephanie ran her tongue across her upper lip. Then she wrapped her arms around his neck, drew his face down toward hers, and gave him a kiss that practically asphyxiated him. By the time he came up for air, half the room was staring at them. "Good-bye, darling," she said.

"Good-bye," said Albie. "Uh, good-bye, Cliff."

Cliff smiled enigmatically. "Good night, big guy."

Albie took one last look at Stephanie and walked back through the house. The couple on the couch was still at it, but he didn't have time to watch. He was in major trouble. It would be easier to turn into a pumpkin than to face Mr. DiPino. Not to mention his mother. Not to mention Jennifer. But Stephanie—ahhh, Stephanie! He would jump through hoops of fire for kisses like that.

His mother's car was parked right where she had said it would be. The lights and the engine were off. Albie opened the back door and looked inside. Sure enough, Jennifer was sitting in the backseat. He scooted in beside her and closed the door.

"Hi, Jennifer. Boy, am I glad to see you. I looked all over."

Jennifer turned and faced him. "Hello, Albie," she said. Her white blouse was soaked across the front. The car reeked of tequila.

Mrs. Jensen started the engine, turned on the lights, and carefully made a U-turn in the gravel driveway. She was onto the main street and heading south before she asked, "Where were you, Albie? It's after eleven."

"Oh, hi Mom. Yeah, I'm really sorry. I was just saying good-bye to some friends, and I completely forgot about the time." His mother's eyes shot poison arrows into the rear-view mirror. But what scared him the most was that she didn't bother to respond.

They rode to Jennifer's house in silence. The smell of tequila was horrible. At first, Albie wondered if Jennifer had gotten drunk with the football player, but she seemed perfectly sober. It was just the big stain on her blouse.

Albie got out and held the door open for Jennifer. She brushed past him and headed up the sidewalk. He was about to get into the front seat when his mother hit him with a poison arrow. "Walk her to the door, Albie." He wasn't going to argue.

They were almost at the porch when the door opened and Mr. DiPino stepped out to meet them. He was wearing a bathrobe and a pair of reading glasses. As Jennifer reached the top step, he placed his hand gently on her shoulder. "Are you all right?" he asked. She just nodded and walked into the house.

Albie stood on the sidewalk, two steps below. Mr. DiPino took off his glasses and stared down at him. The porch light created strange, sharp shadows across his face. The black pupils of his eyes were like empty sockets. *This is it*, Albie thought. *I am dead.*

"Albie," said Mr. DiPino. "You are irresponsible. Jennifer will not be seeing you again." Then he went into the house and closed the door.

Albie stared at the DiPinos' door for a few seconds. When the porch light went out, he turned around and walked back to the car. He got into the front seat and smiled tentatively at his mother. "Hi, Mom."

"Don't you 'Hi, Mom' me. You made that poor girl miserable."

"I'll apologize on Monday. I promise. It's just . . .

Oh, Mom, you have to understand. It's like firecrackers and atom bombs and grand-slam home runs and lightning and thunder and . . ."

"Stop babbling."

"Don't you see? It's a miracle. I'm in love with Stephanie, and Stephanie's in love with me."

ALBIE LEAPED the first three steps in a single bound. He made the next three, and the next, and the next. His body was light; his muscles were strong. He was invincible. He was in love.

He had been thinking about Stephanie all weekend. He kept seeing her face and feeling her breasts and her thigh and imagining what was underneath that skirt. He'd considered calling her on Sunday and asking her to the beach, but he'd decided to play it cool and wait until Monday. And now it was Monday.

As he walked down the hall to Mr. Pierce's room, Albie pictured Stephanie sitting to the right of the semi-circle, far away from Cliff. She'd be wearing shorts, a tight T-shirt, and open-toed sandals. He would sneak up and put his hands over her eyes. "Guess who?" he'd say. Then she'd turn around, flash him a sexy smile, and look right into his eyes.

They probably wouldn't kiss—not in front of the whole Company. On the other hand, maybe they would. After all, she kissed him in front of everyone at the party. Most likely, they would just hold hands and feel the electricity. He would sit beside her and maybe he'd put his arm around her during the session. Afterward, he'd show her his special place in the trees, and they'd make out a little. Then he'd roll his bike with one hand and put the other around her shoulder as they walked down to the lake. After that, anything could happen.

Albie opened the door and walked into the little theater. He looked toward the front of the room. Something was wrong. Stephanie was sitting next to Cliff in the third seat from the left, just where she always sat. Cliff had his arm around her, and they were practically kissing right there in front of everybody. Brent was back in his old seat on the other side of Cliff.

Albie circled around Brent to get a better look at Cliff and Stephanie. They were gazing into each other's eyes and talking with their lips about three millimeters apart.

"Hi," he said. What else was he going to say?

"Hey, Jensen," said Brent. He was still kind of hung over. His eyelids were puffy, and his voice was hoarse from all that howling.

"Big guy," said Cliff. There was something new in his voice—a hint of sarcasm that made "big guy" sound like "asshole."

"Hi, Albie," said Stephanie. He was right about her clothes. Tight T-shirt, shorts—even the sandals. She looked great. But the rest of it wasn't going according to plan. He looked into her eyes for some kind of secret message—a hint—anything. Nothing.

Mr. Pierce entered the room and walked past Albie on his way to the stage. It was time for the session to begin. Albie looked around the semicircle for a place to sit. The only empty chair was between Mitch and Jennifer. Great.

Albie sat down and turned to his right. Mitch didn't even bother to look at him. Maggie leaned over and said hello, though. Good old Maggie. Albie didn't want to look at Jennifer, but he did it anyway. She turned and looked him right in the eyes. Then she smiled. It was like no smile he had ever seen—or felt. The little theater was air-conditioned, but Jennifer's smile felt like absolute zero. 459.67 below. Double-great.

"I have said that memory is divided into two components," Mr. Pierce began. "Sense memory and emotional memory. We have been working on sense memory for the last week, and we will continue to work on it throughout the course. A professional actor might work on sense memory for three or four years."

"That's a lot of showers," said Brent.

"It's not about showers, Brent. I think you know that." Brent closed his puffy eyes and slumped down in his chair. He was too hung over to argue.

"Because our time is so limited, I want to move on to emotional memory. I have always believed that emotional memory is the crowning glory of the Method. While sense work gives reality to our actions and our environment on the stage, emotional work gives reality to our feelings."

"What do you mean 'gives reality to our feelings'?" asked Jennifer. "My feelings are just as real as anybody else's. I don't need to give them reality." The whole Company stared at her. It was a strange outburst, especially for Jennifer. Her voice was loud and strident.

"That's not the point," said Mr. Pierce. "We're talking about your feelings on the stage as you portray the character. In order to reproduce those feelings night after night, the actor must do emotional exercises."

Jennifer looked directly at Mr. Pierce. "I don't get it," she said.

"Bring your chair to the front of the room."

When Jennifer was ready, Mr. Pierce stood to the side like a master of ceremonies. His tone was calm and soothing. "All right, Jennifer, I want you to think back to an experience when you felt a strong and definite emotion."

"Can it be something recent?"

Mr. Pierce smiled. "That's an excellent question. Strasberg felt an emotional memory should be at least seven years in the past in order to separate the actor from the experience. But for a high-school student that would be half a lifetime. So, yes, I'll let you work with something recent."

Jennifer flashed Albie her absolute-zero smile. Then she closed her eyes. "Okay, I'm thinking about it."

"Good," said Mr. Pierce. "Now, don't tell us the emotion or the scene or the events. Just describe the sensations that bring you to the emotion. Do you understand?"

"Yes, I understand." Jennifer sat completely still in the chair. "It is very loud," she said. "And hot. The music is pounding on the inside of my eardrums. People are bumping into me, rubbing up against me. The room is crowded, but I'm completely alone. I don't know anyone. I don't belong. I've been abandoned. Embarrassed. Hurt . . ."

"Sensations," said Mr. Pierce. "Describe the sensations."

"I can feel my heart beating hard in my chest. I'm dripping with sweat. Gasping for breath. There's no air. Too many people. A scratchy beard on a big face is rubbing against my cheeks. It feels like rough sandpaper. Worse. I feel strong muscles holding me, and I smell liquor. Tequila. It's strange and horrible—like perfume made out of gasoline." Jennifer rocked back and forth in the chair. She was breathing hard and her voice was strained. "A cold, hard bottle is pushing against my lips. The smell is nauseating. I try to push it away, but I can't. I'm not strong enough. There's no one to help me. The music is pounding in my ears. I'm screaming, but I can't hear my own voice. The bottle is pushing. Pushing. Pushing. Suddenly I'm wet and smelly and disgusting. Oh God! I hurt so much!"

Jennifer broke into loud, gasping sobs. Her eyes were wide open. Her arms were wrapped around her body as if she was trying to hold herself together. Mr. Pierce knelt beside her and cradled her head against his chest. "There, there, dear," he said. "You'll be all right. I promise you. Everything will be all right."

Scott and Maggie jumped from their seats and gathered around Jennifer, comforting her and holding her in their arms. The other students stared at the scene in silence. Albie stared at the floor. His size twelve glorified gym shoes stared right back. *You're a jerk*, they said. *A complete and absolute jerk*. He rose to his feet and knelt beside Jennifer. She wasn't crying anymore, but her cheeks were streaked with tears. Her breathing was slower.

"I'm sorry," he said. "I'm really sorry. I'm just so sorry."

Jennifer looked back at him through bloodshot eyes. Her tone wasn't cold; it was worse than cold. It was nothing. "Go away, Albie. Leave me alone."

Scott put his arm protectively around her. "I think you've done enough," he said.

"Yeah," said Albie. Mr. Pierce and Maggie looked at him strangely. *Geez, they probably think I'm some kind of monster*. "I'm not the guy with the tequila," he explained. "I promise."

"Sit down, Albert," ordered Mr. Pierce. Maggie didn't say anything.

When Jennifer was feeling better, Scott carried her chair back to the semicircle. Mr. Pierce sat on the edge of the stage. "I'm very sorry this happened," he said. "Unfortunately there's always a danger when we work deeply. I must take responsibility for allowing Jennifer to use such a recent memory. Jennifer, I am truly sorry."

Jennifer tried to smile. Her eyes were still bloodshot, but her tears had dried. She was breathing normally. "That's all right. I wanted to use it. I needed to."

"No," said Mr. Pierce seriously, "it was too raw, too painful. Perhaps many years from now you will think of it again. And then it will work for you."

"Work?" asked Jennifer. "What do you mean?"

Mr. Pierce smiled slightly. "When you need to play inner pain on the stage, you will simply think of tequila."

After the session, Jennifer and Scott stood up quickly and walked toward the door. Albie followed a few steps behind. He didn't bother to be discreet. "Jennifer! Wait!"

Jennifer turned around and stopped him in his tracks. "Just leave me alone." Then she disappeared with Scott.

Albie stood alone in the center of the room. He felt more naked than after his imaginary shower. Marla and Leslie walked by him without a word. They were followed by Mitch and Maggie. Mitch stopped for a moment. His mouth opened slightly as if he were going to say something. Then he shook his head and walked on. Maggie's face was empty. Even the green sparks were gone.

"You hurt her," she said. Then she followed Mitch out the door.

Cliff and Stephanie were talking with Mr. Pierce in front of the stage. Actually, Cliff was talking. Stephanie was running her fingernails along Cliff's arm. Albie walked toward them and stood to the side, waiting for a chance to step in.

"Don't blame yourself," said Cliff. His voice was warm and sincere, as though he were consoling a friend instead of a teacher.

"But I do," Mr. Pierce replied. "I should have stopped her. I should have been more sensitive."

"You are sensitive. You're the most sensitive man I know."

Mr. Pierce smiled, almost blushing. "Thank you, Clifford. That's very kind."

Cliff was about to continue when he noticed Albie. "Hey, big guy—pretty interesting session." It was the new sarcasm.

"Yeah," said Albie, "very interesting."

There was an uncomfortable pause. Stephanie stared at Cliff's arm. "Can I help you, Albert?" asked Mr. Pierce.

"Uh, no," Albie stammered. "I mean, you . . . uh, Stephanie, can I talk to you?"

Stephanie looked up and smiled at Albie like he was a casual friend who dropped by for a chat. "We're talking now, Albie."

"Alone. Please."

She looked at Cliff and then at Mr. Pierce. They were back to their conversation. "Sure, Albie."

Stephanie took a few steps toward the middle of the room. Albie put his hand firmly on her elbow and led her out into the hall. When they were alone, he turned toward her and asked, "What's going on?"

She looked up at him in complete innocence. "What do you mean, Albie?"

"What do I mean? I mean less than forty-eight hours ago, we were making out on the rocks. I mean you kissed me in front of the whole party. I mean . . . geez, Stephanie, you know what I mean."

Stephanie smiled sweetly. "I was drunk, Albie," she said. "I don't remember anything." Then she turned and disappeared into the room.

"Eat your dinner."

"I'm not hungry."

"Are you sick?"

"No, I'm just not hungry."

Mrs. Jensen eyed Albie across the kitchen table. "What's wrong?" she asked.

Albie played with his food. It looked good, but he didn't have an appetite. "Nothing," he said. "Everything."

"How about some dessert? Strawberry ice cream."

"No, really Mom. I'm just not hungry."

"Is there a game on TV?"

Albie shrugged. "They're losers."

Mrs. Jensen took a sip of coffee and set the cup carefully in the center of the saucer. "Do you want to talk about it?" she asked.

Albie shook his head. "No, I mean, yeah. I mean, geez, I don't know what I want."

"Did you apologize to Jennifer?"

"Yeah."

"And?"

Albie stared at his uneaten food. "She told me to leave her alone."

Mrs. Jensen took another sip of coffee. "You hurt her, Albie."

"I know," he said, looking up from his plate. "I didn't mean to. It was just, well, you know—Stephanie. I guess I wasn't thinking straight."

"You weren't thinking at all."

"Yeah."

His mother smiled slightly. "So how's your big romance?"

Albie stared back at his food. It was completely cold now. Dead meatballs. Dead rice. Dead sauce. "It's over," he said. "Everything's over."

Mrs. Jensen rose from her chair and walked around the table. She stood behind Albie and cradled his head against her stomach. "My poor baby," she said. "Poor, poor baby."

"I'm not a baby." He hated to admit it, but it felt good to be held by his mother.

"Yes, you are," she said, gently stroking his hair. "You're a 6'3", almost-sixteeen-year-old baby and you don't know anything."

"What do you mean? What am I supposed to know?"

"How to live."

Albie arched his neck and looked up at his mother.

For once it seemed like she was towering over him. "What are you talking about?"

"I'm talking about being yourself. Be you and be patient. The rest will come."

"Wow, Mom. That's pretty cosmic."

Mrs. Jensen laughed and held her son closer. Then she let him go and walked toward the refrigerator. "Now how about that ice cream?"

Albie pedaled his Peugeot toward the high school. It was a little before noon. The traffic was pretty heavy, but that wasn't a problem. With his long legs he could almost keep up with the cars. He was pedaling hard behind a delivery van when he looked up and saw the Burger Chief about two blocks away. The Chief towered above the buildings, his eyes steady, his warbonnet firmly in place.

Albie pulled out of traffic and cruised along the curb, taking it easy so he could look up at the Chief. There was something about the giant Indian that really got him. He was so tall and strong and serene, always the same, just standing there and offering his burger to the world. He was solid.

Albie pumped his brakes at the edge of the parking lot and glided up to the giant moccasin. He hopped off the bike and knocked down the kickstand. At first he tried to wrap his bicycle chain around the Chief's leg, but it wouldn't quite make it. Finally he locked it through the spokes and around the frame. *What the heck*, he thought, *I can see it through the window.*

Inside, there were a bunch of people from the summer musical. Albie knew most of them, but he wasn't really in the mood for small talk. He went up to the counter and ordered a Chiefburger, onion rings, and a 7-Up. When the food was ready he grabbed an empty booth. He took a big bite out of the burger and washed it down with the soda. It tasted great, but he wasn't very hungry. It was the idea of the Chiefburger that appealed to him. He took another bite and ate a couple of onion rings. Then he played with his food for a while.

Be yourself. Geez, I must be a monster. He took a quick inventory of the casualties. Jennifer hated him. Mitch wasn't talking to him. Maggie was disgusted. Stephanie had amnesia. Cliff was sarcastic. Mr. Pierce liked his shower, but that was all he liked. Brent was friendlier, but so what?

Albie took another halfhearted bite of the Chief-burger and finished his soda. He dumped the leftovers in the trash, headed outside, and unlocked his Peugeot. As he rode over the railroad tracks toward the high school, the midday sun was hot on his back. Sweat ran down the sides of his face and under the collar of his shirt. He parked his bike in the secret spot and went in the back door. The air-conditioning felt cool and comfortable. Mitch was right about that. Mitch was right about a lot of things.

The back stairs were completely silent. Albie took them nice and easy, one at a time. The third-floor hall was empty, too. As he walked toward Mr. Pierce's room, he wondered if he was the only one in the school. It was possible. Anything was possible.

He opened the door and stepped inside. A single light glowed in the ceiling track, creating long mysterious shadows across the room. "Hello," he called tentatively. "Anybody here?" No answer.

He stood for a moment and looked around the little theater. The plastic chairs, the little stage, the musty curtain, the blacked-out windows. It wasn't much, but in the cool shadows of the summer afternoon, it seemed like a sanctuary.

His gaze focused on the stage. The light in the ceiling was shining on a spot in the center of the apron, a few feet from the edge. As if drawn by some magnetic power, Albie walked toward the circle of light. He glanced back toward the door, jumped onto the stage, and stood in the spotlight. He took a deep breath and let it out slowly to relax his muscles. Then he looked out into the shadows of the room as if he were looking into the Danish fog.

"To be, or not to be," he began, "that is the question: Whether 'tis nobler in the mind to suffer . . ." A sound interrupted him. Someone had entered the room.

"Who . . . who is it?" Albie's voice was weak and cracking. His heart was beating hard in his chest. He was completely blinded by the light.

"It's me, Albie. Maggie."

"Oh. Hi." Albie jumped from the stage and sat down in one of the plastic chairs. "Geez, you scared me. I thought you were Mr. Pierce."

Maggie sat down in the chair beside him. "Sorry," she said. "I didn't know you were in the middle of a performance."

Albie shrugged nonchalantly. "I was just fooling around. You're early."

"So are you."

"Where's Mitch?"

"Having a cigarette."

"Oh." They sat for a few moments in silence. Albie could hear Maggie's soft, rhythmic breathing. It was steady and soothing, like waves lapping on the shore.

"Albie, do you mind if I ask you a question—as a friend?"

"Are we friends?"

Maggie turned toward him and touched his hand. "You know we are," she said.

Suddenly his throat felt dry. He stared down at Maggie's hand on his. "Go ahead," he said.

"Why do you keep doing Hamlet's soliloquy?"

"I don't keep doing it."

"You did it at the audition, and you were doing it just now."

Albie shrugged. He was still staring at their hands. "It's a famous speech."

"Of course it is, but it's not your typical high-school-theater stuff. There must be a reason."

He turned toward Maggie and looked into her eyes. The light from the ceiling caught the green sparks. She was beautiful. And he was alone with her. He could feel his heart beating hard in his chest. "It means something," he said.

Maggie leaned closer. Their faces were only a few inches apart. "What does it mean, Albie?"

Albie leaned closer still. Their lips were almost touching. "I don't know," he whispered.

"Zo! I have caught you wiz my woman!" Mitch's

voice boomed across the room. Albie and Maggie broke away from each other and watched him dance across the floor, slicing the air with an imaginary rapier. "I am zee greatest swordsman in all of France," he cried. "I weel avenge my honor! I weel cut off your deek!"

"Great," said Maggie. "One guy thinks he's Hamlet. The other's the Scarlet Pimpernel." She winked at Albie and smiled.

"Just the scarlet pimple," Mitch said, dropping his French accent. "I've got this incredible zit on my neck. Would you mind popping it for me?"

Maggie frowned in disgust. "You are so gross, Mitch."

Mitch shrugged as he sat down beside her. "All boys are gross," he said. "It comes with the equipment. Isn't that right, Albie?"

Albie stared at Mitch. It was the first time they'd spoken in two weeks. "Uh, yeah," he said finally. "I'm totally gross." He paused for a moment. Then he broke into a big smile. "Hi, Mitch."

"Hi, Albie." Mitch was smiling, too.

"What is this," asked Maggie, "a love-in?"

Mitch stood up and put his arm around Albie. "Exactly," he said. "A gross, boyish love-in. No girls allowed."

Maggie shook her head in mock disgust. "I may vomit."

MR. PIERCE STOOD on the far end of the apron, beside the blacked-out windows. A Cheshire-cat smile spread across his face, as if he held some great secret. He paused for dramatic effect. Then, slowly and deliberately, he began to open the old, musty curtain. First a crack, then a foot, then a few feet, then finally the expanse of the proscenium arch. "Voilà!" he said. "The stage!"

Down on the floor, the students sat upright in their seats. There was a feeling of expectation in the room, as if the stage were a magician's hat and a giant rabbit were about to appear.

"Well?" asked Mr. Pierce. "What do you think?"

"I think it's empty," said Brent.

"Very astute," said Mr. Pierce. "Also very stupid."

"I think it's exciting," said Cliff.

Mr. Pierce smiled warmly at Cliff. "As always, Clifford, you have an excellent attitude. But is the stage really exciting? Or is it you?"

For the first time since the sessions began, Cliff seemed stumped for an answer. "I don't really understand," he said.

"You will," said Mr. Pierce. "Come up here." He turned away from Cliff to include the rest of the group. "All of you."

"What are we supposed to do?" asked Scott.

"Whatever you want," said Mr. Pierce. "No rules."

The students looked at each other and got out of their chairs. Most of them walked up the wooden steps, while a few jumped onto the apron. Within a minute there were ten students milling around on the stage. It was barely big enough to hold them. Albie almost bumped into Stephanie. She smiled pleasantly and walked on. As she moved through the other students, he stared at her hips, shifting back and forth with every step. *Geez, I had my hands on those hips. I had my hands on . . .*

Mitch broke Albie's concentration with a whisper, "She did it with the football team, pass it on." Albie started laughing and turned around to find himself looking straight down at Jennifer. She gave him the ice eyes and walked over toward Scott, who was looking at his watch. Maggie was standing in the middle of the stage with her eyes closed, just rocking back and forth. Cliff was trying to get Brent to do a little tap dancing, but Brent wasn't buying it. Leslie and Marla were walking arm in arm, bumping into as many people as possible.

"All right," called Mr. Pierce, "that's enough.

Everybody down." When the students were settled in their chairs, he looked around the semicircle with a little grin on his face. "Well?" he asked.

"Well, what?" asked Marla.

"Well, what is the stage? Is it a place of great tragedy and hilarious comedy? Of gripping drama and outrageous farce? Does it turn mere mortals into the voices of the gods? Does it turn students into artists? How is it different from this world of flesh and blood?"

"It's definitely more crowded," said Albie.

"It's higher," Leslie offered. "I can look down on you for once."

"I like the boards," said Maggie, "the way they feel beneath my feet."

Cliff stretched his arms and sang out, "They make me feel like dancing."

"You always feel like dancing," Brent muttered.

"The wings," said Mitch quietly. "Even on this little stage, I like the secrecy of the wings."

"Yes," Mr. Pierce agreed, "there is something special about the stage. The boards, the wings, the lights, the curtain, the pulleys, and the ropes. But you have not really answered my question. Where is the tragedy and the comedy and the drama and the farce? Where is the power? Where is the art?"

Mr. Pierce pointed at the students one by one. His long, thin finger seemed to reach from the stage to the semicircle of plastic chairs. "If you learn nothing else, learn this," he said. "You are the art. This—" He slapped his hand on the apron, sending a loud *crack!* through the quiet room. "This is nothing but wood."

He paused to let his words sink in. *Geez*, thought

Albie, *he must have been a heck of an actor. Talk about dramatic.*

After a moment, Mr. Pierce looked toward Cliff and smiled. "Clifford, I'd like you to be the first to work on the stage."

Cliff rose to his feet and vaulted onto the apron. He walked toward the center of the stage and waited for further instructions. Mr. Pierce let himself down to the floor and stepped to the side of the semicircle. "All right, Clifford," he said. "First, I want you to strike a regal pose, as if you were a great king."

Cliff stood to his full height and tilted his head back slightly, lifting his nose and jaw in the air. He expanded his chest and held his right arm a few feet in front of his body, as though he were holding a scepter. The expression on his face was a cross between a regal sneer and a proud smile.

Maggie cupped her hand and whispered into Albie's ear, "Like a Greek god."

"Excellent," said Mr. Pierce. "Now I want you to hold that same feeling and become a lion."

"A what?" asked Cliff. He was losing his royal composure.

"A lion," Mr. Pierce repeated. "Crouch on the stage and pose like a regal lion."

Cliff broke out of character for a moment and smiled at Mr. Pierce. "Interesting," he said. Regaining his concentration, he slowly eased himself into a squat. Then he folded his fingers into his palms, leaned forward, and supported himself on his hands. His head was erect, and his face once again held the sneer-smile.

"Like a Greek lion," Maggie whispered. Albie

turned toward her and held his finger to his lips. He was on the verge of laughing.

"All right," said Mr. Pierce. "You are now a lion in a cage."

Cliff held his lion pose for a moment. Then he turned his head from side to side, as though he were looking around the cage. Suddenly, he opened his mouth and roared at the top of his lungs. The blacked-out windows shook with the sound. Some of the students laughed, but it wasn't funny—it was just so surprising. When the roar died, Cliff moved around the stage on his hands and legs. He was slinky and strong and menacing. His movements clearly defined the limits of the cage.

Maggie leaned closer to Albie. "The Greek lion can almost act," she whispered.

"Excellent," said Mr. Pierce. "Now we will add the final ingredient. The door of the cage is open. How will you approach this? Speak to me as the lion."

Cliff returned to his lion pose in the center of the stage. He closed his eyes and considered the question. "Confusion," he said. His voice was hoarse and gravelly—half-human, half-lion.

"Confusion?" asked Mr. Pierce. "Are you sure?"

Cliff looked down at the students; his eyes were wild and hungry. For a moment, his focus rested on Stephanie. She gazed at him as though she wanted to jump into the cage and be his lioness. He turned away from her and looked back toward Mr. Pierce. "The lion is confused," he said.

"Play that confusion."

"Where is the door?"

Mr. Pierce gestured toward the front of the stage. "Here, in front of me."

Cliff closed his eyes and concentrated. When he was ready, he began to move around the cage. He was restless and agitated. Occasionally he roared, but they were not strong, regal roars. They were weak and frustrated, like the pitiful whines of a big alley cat. When he passed the area in front of Mr. Pierce, he put his paw tentatively through the imaginary opening. Then he pulled it back and paced again. Each time he passed the open door, he reached his paw a little farther into the outside world. Then he withdrew it and paced again.

The students watched in fascination. Cliff was no longer *acting* like a lion—he *was* a lion. For a moment, Albie forgot that Cliff was Cliff or that the stage was completely bare. He saw the cage and the door. He felt the confusion of the lion. Would he walk through the open door? Would he? Would he?

"Bravo," said Mr. Pierce, cutting off the scene. "A fine performance." The entire Company applauded enthusiastically as Cliff stepped off the stage and sat down. Maggie smiled at Albie. "The Greek lion *can* act," she said. Even Mitch was impressed. He was whistling through his teeth and stomping his feet. Everyone expected Cliff to do a good job, but this was something new, something real.

"You didn't give him enough time," said Marla.

"He's still in the cage," said Albie.

Mr. Pierce smiled. "We'll have to wait for the sequel. Now, which of Clifford's little scenes was the most dramatic?"

"The last one," said Scott. "Obviously."

"Yes," said Mr. Pierce. "Obviously. And would you also agree that each scene was better than the one before?"

"Yes."

"Good. Now tell me this. What changed between the king and the lion, the lion and the cage, the cage and the open door? Did the stage change?"

"No, the stage was always the same."

"Precisely." Mr. Pierce gazed at Cliff like an artist appreciating his own work. "The only thing that changed was Clifford."

ALBIE LOOKED OUT the window of the El as it clattered into the city. Run-down brick apartment buildings rushed by like old, tired monsters. Laundry hung in tiny backyards, and men in undershirts drank beer on wooden steps. Children danced around an open fire hydrant, splashing and sliding in the street. It was Saturday, and it was hot.

Mitch sat beside him, his boots propped on the seat in front. He looked straight ahead, an unlit cigarette dangling from his mouth. No Smoking signs were plastered up and down the car.

Suddenly, the El took a wide turn toward the east. This was the part Albie liked best. To the right was an old cemetery. The tombstones were worn white with age, and bright graffiti covered the outside walls. To the left were modern high-rise apartments and condominiums. Beyond the high rises, he could see the lake, sparkling in the summer sunlight.

"We should've gone swimming," he said.

Mitch looked at him as if he'd been interrupted. "Huh?"

"It's so hot. Maybe we should've gone swimming instead."

Mitch took the cigarette out of his mouth and rolled it slowly between his fingers. "Naw, we can go swimming anytime. This is special."

"What's it all about anyway?"

"I told you. It's a parade."

"What kind of parade?"

"Just a neighborhood thing. You'll see." Mitch stuck the cigarette back in his mouth and looked toward the front of the train.

"Too bad Maggie couldn't come," said Albie.

"Yeah."

Albie went back to the window. *Yeah. Too bad you're not Maggie.* It was terrible, but it was true. He was a traitor to his best friend. It was great to be with Mitch, but he kept seeing Maggie's eyes, and hearing her voice, and feeling the touch of her hand. It was like Stephanie, only worse. Or better. Or both.

At the next stop, Mitch swung his boots to the floor and stood up. "This is where we get off."

Albie stood up, grabbed the bar overhead, and slid out into the aisle. Mitch was already waiting at the door. Albie worked his way through the crowd and stood beside him. When the door opened, the surge of people pushed them out onto the platform. Once they were down on the street, Mitch lit his cigarette and took a long drag. Then he led them toward the east. After a few blocks, they turned onto a wide street lined with stores and restaurants. Hundreds of people were already standing along the curb, waiting for the parade to begin.

"This is it," Mitch said. "I guess we just find a spot where we can see."

"I can see from anywhere."

"That's because you're a mutation."

"Maybe if you stopped smoking, you'd start growing."

Mitch took a puff of his cigarette. "I've been the same height since eighth grade."

"When did you start smoking?"

"Eighth grade."

"Hey, I think it's starting!" On tiptoe, Albie could see clearly over the crowd standing along the curb. There was something happening farther down the block. The traffic had stopped, and a policeman was directing cars away from the street. Mitch pushed through the crowd to get a better view. Albie just stayed on his toes.

The parade began with a drum majorette in a sparkly, spangly uniform. She high-stepped up the street, swinging her baton in time to the music. The sound blared from a loudspeaker somewhere behind him. It wasn't normal parade music—it was more like something out of a dance club. The beat was hot and the drum majorette was right with it. Albie stretched a little higher to get a good look at her. She had a great pair of legs.

The majorette was followed by two more girls in

sparkly, spangly outfits. They were carrying a long white banner between them. As the banner approached, the crowd began to applaud and cheer. Albie looked over the heads of the people to read the sign. In bright multicolored letters, it said: GAY PRIDE PARADE. Albie stared at the words as if they were written in a foreign language. *What the heck is a Gay Pride Parade?* He read the banner again and then again. Suddenly it hit him right between the eyes. *These people are a bunch of fags!*

As the banner passed directly in front of him, he got a close look at one of the girls in the sparkly, spangly uniforms. Only she wasn't a girl—she was a man. It was eleven in the morning, but he already had a five o'clock shadow. Albie looked toward the drum majorette disappearing down the street. *No. It can't be.* He ran back up the street to see her from the front again. It was true. The majorette was a man.

Albie stared at the faces in the crowd. He hadn't really noticed before, but now it was obvious. They were almost all men. Some of them had their arms around each other. Some were holding hands. Some were even kissing. There were a few women, too. But the men were standing with men, and the women were standing with women. *They're all fags. Fags and lesbos.*

He walked back to his original position and looked around for Mitch. He couldn't find him in the crowd. *What the heck. They're not gonna bite me. I might as well watch the parade.*

After the banner came eight acrobats in tights and leotards doing cartwheels and somersaults and back flips right down the street. The sound truck was next, followed by a bunch of guys on motorcycles dressed completely in black leather. Then there were some guys in hard hats with white undershirts and cigarette packs rolled under their sleeves. When they got closer, Albie realized the guys were girls. They were followed by some real guys in fancy dresses with make-up and feather boas. Their make-up was running like crazy in the heat, but they seemed to think the whole thing was hysterical. Then there were some pretty regular looking women walking arm-in-arm, smiling and waving to the crowd. The last group was a bunch of regular-looking guys who were all hugging and waving and laughing and having a great time.

As the marchers passed, some of the people from the crowd stepped out into the street and followed behind. For a while, the parade seemed to be going backward and forward at the same time, as more and more people poured into the street. Finally, the line of marchers moved past Albie's position. As he watched them disappear down the street, he could still hear the dance-club march blaring in the distance.

"Well?" Mitch was standing beside him. "What did you think of the parade?"

Albie looked again toward the disappearing marchers. "Geez," he said, "I don't know."

Mitch smiled. "Are you glad we came?"

Albie shrugged. "Yeah, sure. I mean, I don't want you to think I'm a fag or anything."

Mitch shook his head. "I don't think you're a fag."

"Where'd you hear about this, anyway?"

"I read about it in the paper. Y'wanna go get something to drink? I'm dying of thirst."

"Sure."

They walked for a couple of blocks, threading their way through the crowd. There were still hundreds of people on the sidewalk, but they were gradually filtering into the shops and restaurants and bars. Albie noticed a familiar figure walking into a clothing store a few yards ahead—tall, thin, and pale.

"Mr. Pierce!"

Mr. Pierce turned around at the sound of Albie's voice. He flashed a nervous smile and stepped back out of the store and onto the sidewalk. His shirt was unbuttoned halfway down his chest, revealing a few thin hairs. Sweat was running down the side of his face. "Albert," he said. "Mitchell. How nice to see you."

Albie stood face-to-face with Mr. Pierce. It was always weird to meet a teacher outside of school, but this was *really* weird. "Did you see the parade?" he asked.

Mr. Pierce glanced uncomfortably back into the store. "The parade?" he asked. "What parade?"

"The Gay Pride Parade," said Mitch.

Mr. Pierce glanced again into the store. "Uh, no. I'm afraid I didn't have the opportunity to see that. Well, boys, it was very nice to see you, but I must run. I'm doing some shopping for . . . costumes."

He was about to walk into the store when a tan, muscular figure appeared in the doorway. It was Cliff.

"Dale," he said, addressing Mr. Pierce, "what are you . . ."

Mr. Pierce cleared his throat nervously. "Clifford, Albert and Mitchell are here."

Cliff stopped in his tracks and looked at Albie. For an instant, his tan, handsome face lost its color. He looked down at Mitch and up at Mr. Pierce. Then he looked back at Albie. "Hi, big guy," he said. No sarcasm this time.

"Cliff," said Albie.

"Imagine meeting you here," said Mitch.

"Clifford was kind enough to help me look for costumes," explained Mr. Pierce.

"Costumes," said Albie vacantly.

"Well," Mr. Pierce continued, "it was so nice to see you boys, but we really must be going." He nodded toward Cliff, and the two of them walked quickly up the street. Albie and Mitch watched them disappear in the same direction as the parade.

"How can they buy costumes when we don't even have a show?" asked Albie.

"Good question," said Mitch.

"Maybe it's for another show."

"Maybe."

There was an old-fashioned ice-cream parlor in the middle of the next block. It was decorated like something out of the 1890s, with wicker ceiling fans slowly circulating the air. On the walls there were posters of Marilyn Monroe, Bette Davis, and Joan Crawford. Two women sat at a small table in the back—the rest of the customers were men. Albie and Mitch found two open stools at the counter. The waiter smiled at Albie and sort of tossed his head and shimmied his body. "What'll it be, honey?" he asked.

Albie shifted on his stool. "Well, uh, I'd like a root beer float."

"One black cow." The waiter looked at Mitch.

"Iced coffee, please. And a tall glass of water."

The waiter glanced at Albie and turned back to Mitch with a sly smile. "It looks to me like you've already got the tall drink of water," he said. Then he whirled around and walked toward the order window, swinging his hips back and forth all the way.

"Geez," said Albie.

"He's having a good time," said Mitch.

"Yeah, but . . ."

"They're not all like that, y'know."

"I know, but still . . ."

Mitch shrugged. "Different strokes for different folks."

When the waiter brought their drinks, he winked at Albie and sashayed away. The guy was starting to get on his nerves. But what really bothered him was Cliff and Mr. Pierce.

"Mitch?"

"Yeah?"

"Do you think it's possible?"

"Do I think what's possible?"

"Cliff . . . and Mr. Pierce."

Mitch sipped his iced coffee and followed it with a long drink of water. "I don't know," he said. "I suppose anything's possible."

Albie stirred his black cow. "That's what my mother says."

"I gotta admit," Mitch continued, "if it *is* true, he's been putting up one hell of a front."

"Yeah," said Albie, eating a spoonful of ice cream. "A hell of a front. I mean there's Stephanie and the girl in green, and Cliff is such a—you know—masculine guy. He's built like a brick, and he's got hair on his chest like you wouldn't believe."

"Being hairy is not queer insurance."

"Yeah, well, you know what I mean."

Mitch took another sip of his coffee. Then he finished off the water. "Yeah. I know what you mean."

"It's impossible," Albie said finally. "There must be another explanation."

"I'm gay," said Mitch.

"Maybe I'll ask him. Sort of casual, y'know—like, 'Hey, Cliff, did you find your costumes?' I'm sure he can explain it." Albie dipped his spoon into the black cow. His favorite part was when the ice cream melted into the root beer.

Mitch reached over and placed his hand on top of Albie's, stopping him as he dipped into the float. Albie turned toward him. Mitch's face was very serious. "Albie, did you hear what I said?" he asked.

"Geez, Mitch. I'm sorry. I was—you know—thinking about Cliff and everything."

"I said, I'm gay."

Albie's face broke into a grin. "C'mon, Mitch. Cut the shit. I mean, normally, I would think it was hysterical, but right now it makes me kind of nervous."

Mitch dropped his hand from Albie's, but he continued looking directly into his eyes. "I'm sorry that it makes you nervous, Albie. But I want you to know. I'm gay. I'm queer. I'm a faggot. I'm a homosexual. This is not a joke. This is my life."

Albie pushed his root beer float to the side. "You're

not kidding?" he asked. Except it wasn't really a question.

Mitch looked down at his coffee. "No," he said.

They sat together quietly for a while. Albie looked at the movie posters on the walls and the ceiling fans turning slowly above their heads. He watched the gay waiter run up and down the counter, dishing out sundaes and sodas and shakes and banana splits. He watched the gay customers, eating and laughing at the tables. Finally, he turned toward Mitch and asked, "Why are you telling me this?"

Mitch looked up from his coffee and gazed directly into Albie's eyes. "I need to," he said.

"How do you know? I mean, about being . . . you know . . . gay?"

"I know. Believe me."

"Have you told your parents?"

Mitch turned away and looked down at the counter. "No," he said.

"What about Maggie?"

"She was the first to know."

"Oh." *Geez. I guess everybody's putting up a hell of a front. Everybody except me.*

"Y'wanna know something funny?" Mitch asked.

"What's that?"

"The whole thing with you. Burger Chief and being friends—at least in the beginning—that was all her idea."

"You're kidding."

"No, Albie. I'm not kidding."

"Wow—that's great! I mean, geez . . . well, you know . . ."

Mitch smiled. "Yes, Albie. I know."

They sat for a while longer at the counter. Mitch finished his coffee, and Albie played around with his black cow. The waiter brought their bill. They put their money on the counter, but there was no rush to walk out into the hot city street. The ice-cream parlor was cool and comfortable. Albie kept looking back and forth between Mitch and the other customers, trying to find some magical connection between them. Mitch looked straight ahead.

"Albie," he said, "there's something I want to ask you, and I want you to be completely honest. Will you do that?"

"Sure."

Mitch ran his finger around the lip of his glass, as though he expected it to start making music. "Are we still friends?"

Albie listened for the sound of the glass. He could barely hear it in the noisy ice-cream parlor. But it was there—a gentle, high-pitched whistle. He reached out and covered Mitch's hand with his own. "You know we are."

ALBIE GAZED LONGINGLY at Maggie. She was standing a few feet away, smiling sweetly, waiting patiently. Behind him, he could feel Stephanie's hot, angry presence.

"You'll never leave me," Stephanie shouted. "You don't have the courage."

"I must," he said. "I have no choice."

"Are you ready?" asked Maggie. Her voice was sweet and musical.

"Choice?" hissed Stephanie. "What do you know about choice. You're spineless. I made you."

"I love her," said Albie. He was still looking at Maggie, but his body was turning toward Stephanie.

"I love you," said Maggie. Her voice was fading away, as if a mist had fallen between them.

"Love!" cried Stephanie. "What do you know about love?"

He could feel her approaching him from behind. Her hot breath was on his neck. His body was turning. Maggie was fading. Now he was face-to-face with Stephanie. She ran her tongue across her upper lip. Then she wrapped her arms around his neck. "This is what you know," she said. Fiercely, violently, she pulled him toward her and kissed him deeply on the mouth. He could feel her pressing against him. His blood was pumping through his veins. He was lost. He was hers.

"Cut!" said Mr. Pierce. "That will be enough."

Stephanie broke away from Albie and smiled pleasantly. "Hope I didn't asphyxiate you," she said. Then she turned around and descended the wooden steps from the stage. Maggie stood near the wing. The sweet patience on her face was replaced by a bemused smile. "Lust beats love every time," she said. Then she returned to her seat. Albie was alone in the center of the stage. He was still breathing hard.

"Cross your legs," Mitch suggested.

Albie looked down at his pants. It wasn't really obvious, but he was embarrassed anyway.

"Come now, Albert," Mr. Pierce chided. "An actor must exercise control. Please return to your seat."

Albie jumped off the stage and sat down. He gave Mitch a light dig in the ribs. "Thanks a lot," he said. Then he turned to Maggie. "I couldn't help it," he whispered.

She wouldn't look at him. "Uh-huh," she said. It was hard to tell whether she was really mad or just teasing.

"Comments?" asked Mr. Pierce.

"It was good," said Scott. "Stephanie was completely believable. I think it's the best work she's done."

"She was born for the part," said Cliff. He was back to sarcasm.

"Maggie was good, too," offered Marla. "She didn't have as much to do, but she played it perfectly. It almost seemed like she and Stephanie were two sides of the same woman."

"I agree," said Mr. Pierce. "I thought they had an interesting dynamic. I'd like to see them work more together. What about Albert?"

"He was better in the shower," said Brent.

"A cold shower," added Cliff.

"That's not fair. It was a difficult part. He had to play between them." Jennifer's voice was quiet, but strong. It was the first time she'd spoken in class since her breakdown.

"I agree," said Mitch. "Albie had a nice sense of tension. He demonstrated it through his body more than his words."

"The tension was good," agreed Mr. Pierce, "but Albert was the weak link in the chain. The two women were very strong. He allowed himself to be tossed between them like a ship at sea. He never took control."

"But that was the part," said Albie.

Mr. Pierce shook his head. "No, Albert, that was your interpretation of the part. A different actor might have created a different ending."

As Albie slumped further in his seat, Mr. Pierce lifted himself up to the edge of the stage and made himself comfortable. He took off his coat and laid it beside him. Then he loosened his tie and rolled up his sleeves. His face and arms were sunburned from the hot weekend.

"Don't look so depressed, Albert," he said pleasantly. "It's only an exercise. If you want to become an actor, you must deal with criticism. Now, if there are no more comments, I'd like to discuss our final show."

"It's about time," said Scott.

"Yeah," Brent agreed.

"Let's do something different," Maggie suggested.

"We've only got two weeks," Marla said.

"Listen," Mr. Pierce commanded. "Please. I have given this a great deal of thought. We don't have time to rehearse a full-length show. That was never our purpose. However, we must create a performance worth watching." He paused and looked around the semicircle. "You know that I believe in the creative spark. That's why I became an actor. That's why I'm teaching the Method. But I also believe that every audience has a built-in crap detector. It's fine to take a shower or to be a lion in an acting exercise. It's nonsense to do it in front of an audience who expects a coherent and professional show."

"So what do we do?" asked Scott.

Mr. Pierce smiled slightly. "An evening of scenes. Very simple. Very straightforward."

"What kind of scenes?" asked Maggie.

"I will leave that up to you. You may work on an old scene using our new techniques. Or you may work on something completely new. But, whatever you choose, it should be something you can really sink your teeth into."

"Are we wearing costumes?" Mitch asked. His voice was perfectly casual.

Mr. Pierce looked nervously over at Cliff and then back at Mitch. "Well, yes," he said. "You may use costumes if you feel they're necessary. Nothing elaborate, though. The same goes for sets. We'll keep it as simple as possible. Let the audience concentrate on the acting."

The room buzzed with the students' voices as they began discussing possible scenes.

"Well," said Mitch, "what do you think?"

Albie stared at Stephanie, who was talking with Cliff and Mr. Pierce. He could still feel her body pressing against him. "About what?" he asked.

Mitch looked up at him in exasperation. "About our policies in Central America," he said.

"Geez," said Albie, "I don't know . . ." *It's just acting—illusion. It's Maggie I want. But still . . .*

"The scene, shit-for-brains! What do you wanna do for our scene?"

Albie looked down at Mitch. "Oh, uh . . . I figured you and Maggie would do something."

Mitch shook his head. "She's doing something with Stephanie."

"You're kidding."

"Have I ever lied to you?"

Albie looked back at Stephanie. Sure enough, there was Maggie talking a mile a minute. "I thought she hated Stephanie."

"Pierce wants them to work together."

"What about Cliff?"

"Evidently he has other plans."

Cliff was still talking with Mr. Pierce. They were laughing and gesturing as though they were planning a party. Brent stood beside them, waiting to be included in the conversation.

"Geez . . . it's true, isn't it, Mitch? I mean, Cliff and Mr. Pierce."

Mitch shrugged. "I don't know, Albie. I don't have a built-in queer detector." His voice was pitched softly so the others wouldn't hear.

Albie glanced at him in surprise. "I thought, well . . . you know."

Mitch smiled. "You thought we all had secret homosexual decoder rings. We get 'em in Crackerjack boxes."

Albie laughed. "I guess that was kind of stupid, huh?"

Mitch stepped toward the blacked-out windows so they could continue the discussion in privacy. "Listen, Albie, I'm too busy with my own life to worry about Cliff. But, if you want my opinion, Cliff is looking for something and he thinks that Pierce just might have it."

"What does he want?"

"Ask Cliff."

Albie looked over at Cliff and Mr. Pierce. They were really excited now. Even Brent was getting into the act.

"I don't think so," said Albie. "We're not really friends."

"I'm sorry to hear that. So what about the scene?"

"Huh?"

"The scene, doofus! What are we gonna do?"

Albie gazed into the blacked-out window. It was

like a dark, smoky mirror. *Geez, this is not easy.* "Look, Mitch," he said, turning away from the window, "we *are* friends. It doesn't bother me that you're gay. I mean, sure, it sort of surprised me, but if that's who you are, that's who you are. I accept that. But I don't want to do a scene with you."

"Nice friend," Mitch muttered.

"It has nothing to do with friendship. It's just that there's something else I want to do. I have to talk to Pierce."

"You wanta do a scene with Pierce?"

"I want to do something by myself."

"By yourself? Why the hell would you wanta . . ." Mitch stopped in the middle of his sentence and stared at Albie in amazement. *"Hamlet,"* he said. "You wanta do goddamn *Hamlet.*"

Albie shrugged.

"You're nuts," said Mitch.

"Maybe."

"He'll never let you do it."

"I have to ask."

"No, Albert. Absolutely not." Mr. Pierce was sitting on the edge of the stage. Albie stood beside him. The rest of the students had left for the day.

"Why not?"

"It's too difficult. You're only fifteen years old."

"Almost sixteen."

"Whatever. Remember what I said about professionalism. Sometimes it's better to shoot a little lower and hit a little higher. Do you understand what I mean?"

"No, sir. Not really."

"Hamlet's soliloquy is the most famous dramatic speech in the English language. Everybody's heard it and seen it performed a million times. An actor must be extraordinary to carry it off. Look at yourself, Albert! You could barely hold your own in the little improvisation."

"I wasn't that bad."

"You weren't that good."

Albie looked away from Mr. Pierce toward the blacked-out windows. From this distance there was no reflection. No dark smoke. Just blackness. "I want to do it," he said.

"Why, Albert?"

"It means something . . . the words. Geez, I don't know."

"That's not good enough, Albert."

"They really get me. Inside."

"The answer is no."

Albie turned away from the windows and stared directly into Mr. Pierce's eyes. He spoke very slowly and steadily, enunciating each word. "Maybe I want to do it for the same reason that you and Cliff were looking for costumes . . . sir."

Mr. Pierce recoiled as if he had been slapped across the face. His eyebrows arched toward his forehead, and his jaw snapped back toward his shoulder. "Are you trying to blackmail me, Albert?"

Albie was still staring into the teacher's eyes. "No, but I want to do the soliloquy."

Mr. Pierce took a deep breath and smiled slightly.

"All right, Albert. I will give you permission to make an ass of yourself. But you must promise me something."

"Anything."

"Bring something new to the part. I don't care what it is, but for God's sake make it different."

ALBIE MOVED TOWARD the center of the stage. The light shone brightly in his eyes, but that didn't matter. He wasn't on a hot wooden stage at Wilmont High School. He was in a cold, damp Danish castle. He shivered and tensed his muscles against the northern night. Then he released the tension ever so slightly, shrinking his tall, gawky frame. This Hamlet was no high school basketball player. He was a prince.

"To be, or not to be," he began, "that is the question: Whether 'tis nobler in the mind to suffer the slings and arrows of outrageous fortune or to take arms against a sea of troubles, and by opposing end them. To die— to sleep—no more . . ."

As the speech progressed, Albie moved onto the apron of the stage. He was wearing black loafers, tight black jeans, and a white shirt with flowing sleeves. They were just old clothes that his mother had fixed up, but they helped him get into the Shakespearean spirit. The sleeves were the best. He loved the way they ruffled through the air when he wanted to accentuate a line.

"For who would bear the whips and scorns of time, the oppressor's wrong, the proud man's contumely, the pangs of despised love . . ."

For the bare bodkin, Albie had taken an old, dull kitchen knife and sprayed it with silver paint. It looked pretty good from a distance. As he spoke the words, he held the knife in his hand and ran his thumb thoughtfully along the edge of the blade. ". . . when he himself might his quietus make with a bare bodkin?"

By the end of the soliloquy, Albie was back in the center of the stage. He looked toward the wing, as if someone were about to enter. "Soft you now!" he cried. "The fair Ophelia!"

As the lights faded, there were a few quick hand claps from the other students. It wasn't really applause, but that didn't mean anything. After all, it was dress rehearsal, and they were busy preparing for their own scenes. When the stage was completely dark, Albie walked into the wing and down the wooden steps.

The little theater was already set up for the performance. Neat rows of plastic chairs filled most of the room. There was an aisle from the door leading toward the wooden steps and another aisle along the windows. Mr. Pierce sat in the back row, taking notes on a clipboard. Behind him, one of the tech kids was working the lightboard.

As Albie left the stage, Mr. Pierce gestured toward

him. *Great, here it comes.* Albie walked along the wall and around the back of the room toward the lightboard. Then he leaned over so Mr. Pierce could talk to him without disturbing the next scene.

"Albert, I'd like to speak with you after the rehearsal. Privately."

"Yes, sir. Is there something I can work on?"

Mr. Pierce's eyes were glued to the stage. Even in the dark theater, his face glowed with satisfaction, as if he were looking at a beautiful painting. "Not now," he said. "Later." *Of course,* Albie thought. *It's Cliff's scene.*

As Albie walked back toward the front of the theater, he watched Cliff and Brent begin their scene. It was the opening of *Waiting for Godot.* The stage was completely bare except for a surrealistic tree that stood black and gnarled in the hot lights. Mr. Pierce had gotten some stagecraft kids to come in and build it.

Albie slipped into a chair next to Maggie. She was still in the long gown she wore as the Dowager Empress in *Anastasia.* It was just something she found lying around in the costume room, but it made her look very grand and stately. She had a little old-age make-up on her face. Nothing heavy—just a few lines here and there. Most of the age had to come from within.

"Hi," Albie whispered.

"Hi yourself," Maggie whispered back.

"I'm really bad, aren't I?"

"Of course not. What gave you that idea?"

"Pierce. He wants to talk to me privately."

"That doesn't mean you're bad."

"It doesn't mean I'm good."

In the back row, Mr. Pierce cleared his throat. It was just loud enough to give them an unmistakable "quiet" signal, but not loud enough to disturb the players on the stage. Albie and Maggie smiled at each other like two kids staying up past their bedtime. In the dim theater, his suspicions were confirmed once and for all: The green sparks in Maggie's eyes really did glow in the dark.

Onstage, Cliff and Brent were walking around the surrealistic tree saying surrealistic, existential things. They were dressed as hoboes with bowler hats. They were supposed to be waiting for Godot, who was supposed to be some sort of God figure. It was a pretty cool play, really. Of course, it was Mr. Pierce's idea.

When the scene was over, Albie and Maggie went back to their conversation. The final scene would take a couple of minutes to set up. It was Marla, Leslie, and Mitch in *The Glass Menagerie*.

"Maggie," said Albie, "I want you to look me in the eyes and tell me I'm good."

"Albie, that's so silly."

"Please. It would mean a lot to me."

Maggie covered her mouth with her hand to stop from laughing. "Albie . . ."

"See, you can't do it. I can do it for you. Watch: Maggie, you are good. No, I can go even further. Maggie, you are great. Stephanie is good. You are great. Your scene is almost as great as you are. There, see. No problem."

Maggie pulled her hand away from her face. Her

smile was more serious. "Albie, that's really sweet of you."

Albie shook his head. "It's not sweet. It's true."

They sat silently for a moment. On the dark stage, they could hear the rough sliding of furniture being moved into place.

"You *are* good," Maggie said finally. "It's just . . ."

"Just what?"

"Hard. It's so hard what you're doing. I mean, you're all alone up there. You're doing *Hamlet*. God, I couldn't do it."

"Yes, you could."

"No, I couldn't. None of us could."

Onstage, the lights were slowly rising on an apartment in St. Louis. It was the 1930s, the heart of the Depression. The set was simple—a table, a few chairs, a sofa, a picture on the wall. As Mitch stumbled drunkenly onto the stage, Albie thought back to the night of the whiskey. Even then—when he really was drunk—Mitch never acted stupid. Now it was the same. He acted drunk all right, but he wasn't stupid.

Mitch reached into his pocket for a key and moved his hand unsteadily toward the door. Just as he was about to insert it into the lock, the key slipped from his fingers and clattered to the ground. He bent over, hovering a few inches above the stage. He had incredible control of his body. Pinpoint concentration. But it was more than that. He was reaching from the inside out.

As Albie watched the scene progress, he felt a smile creeping over his face. He glanced at Maggie and she was smiling, too. It wasn't that the scene was funny—

parts of it were pretty depressing. It was just that Mitch was so darn good. Sometimes, Albie couldn't even remember that he was Mitch. And, of course, he really wasn't Mitch. He was Tom Winfield.

When the scene was over, the little theater erupted in applause. The ovation continued for a couple of minutes. It was pretty amazing considering that there were only nine people in the audience. But it wasn't just for *The Glass Menagerie*. It was for the whole show, the whole six weeks, the whole Company.

"All right," said Mr. Pierce. "Everyone to the front row."

Maggie was about to get up and move toward the front, when Albie reached out and placed his hand over her wrist. His long fingers curled all the way around and touched the heel of his hand. "Maggie," he said, "could I ask you something?"

Maggie smiled and sat back down in her chair. "Of course, Albie. Is it about *Hamlet?*"

He could tell by the look on her face that she was hoping it wasn't. "Forget *Hamlet*. I was just, uh, wondering if maybe you would, uh, like to maybe go to, uh, Burger Chief after rehearsal? I mean, I have to talk to Mr. Pierce for a few minutes, and I know it's late and we could ask Mitch and I completely understand if you can't, but . . ."

"I'd love to, Albie."

Albie smiled at her. With the lights up, he realized that the green in her gown went with the green in her eyes. "Great, Maggie. That's really great. I'll go ask Mitch."

"Do you want to ask Mitch?"

"Do you want me to ask Mitch?"

"Forget Mitch."

Albie sat next to Mr. Pierce in the front row of the little theater. A single light was shining on the apron of the stage. Maggie was waiting out in the hall. The rest of the students were gone.

"Albert," said Mr. Pierce, "before we discuss your scene, I want to make something very clear."

"Yes, sir?" Albie's heart was beating quickly.

"You will not make an ass of yourself."

Albie smiled and let out a long, slow breath. "Thank you," he said. "I'm glad to hear that. Very glad."

"You've done some good work, Albert. There is a strong sense of place and temperature. Unlike many Hamlets I've seen, you seem to understand that he is the Prince of Denmark."

"That's because I'm Danish."

"That's good. If it works, use it. You also do a nice job on the poetry. You've obviously spent a great deal of time on this."

"Hours," said Albie. "Hours and hours and . . ."

"But," said Mr. Pierce.

"But?"

"But . . . the question I keep asking myself is why?"

"Why?"

"Yes, why, Albert? Remember professionalism? Remember the crap detector? Here we have a tight, powerful evening of scenes. Maggie and Stephanie start it off with an emotional bang. Jennifer and Scott lighten it up a bit. Then all of a sudden this big geek walks out and does Hamlet's soliloquy. What's the point?"

Albie stared ahead toward the stage. "Maybe we should change the order."

"That will not solve the problem."

There was a long pause. "Am I really a big geek?" he asked.

"I'm sorry, Albert. That was an unfortunate choice of words."

"I try to shrink."

"Don't bother," said Mr. Pierce. "You will always be tall."

"And skinny."

"I'm afraid so. Listen to me, Albert. I have learned this from painful experience. Tall, thin actors look even taller and thinner on stage. Particularly a small stage. You look like you're scraping the ceiling."

"Is that so bad?"

"It's strange. People expect something different."

Albie stared down at his long legs, stretching into the shadows. Mr. Pierce's legs stretched beside him. They were the same length.

"You're tall," said Albie.

"And thin."

"But you were an actor."

Mr. Pierce laughed quietly. "I am a teacher."

"Geez . . . the show's tomorrow."

"I know, Albert. And I have only myself to blame. I should never have allowed you to play the part. But you promised me to be different."

"I thought I was."

Mr. Pierce shook his head wearily. "No, Albert, you are competent, but you are not different." There was silence in the little theater. Albie stared at the tips of his black Hamlet shoes. "Tell me, Albert," said Mr. Pierce, "what is the meaning of the soliloquy?"

Albie thought for a moment. He knew the speech inside out, but he was afraid to answer too quickly. "He's trying to decide whether or not he should kill himself."

"And what does he decide?"

"He decides not to. He puts the bodkin away."

"Why?"

"He's afraid of what might happen after death."

"Have you ever wanted to kill yourself, Albert?"

Albie looked at Mr. Pierce in surprise. "No. I mean, I've been really depressed, but I always figured something would work out."

Mr. Pierce smiled. "That's an admirable attitude. What have you been using as your emotional memory?"

Albie looked toward the blacked-out windows. "There was this time when I was just a little kid," he said. "It's kind of hard to talk about."

"Go ahead, Albert."

"Well, uh, my father had just left us and my mother and I were living in this little apartment and—I don't know—it just seemed really bleak and depressing."

"It's not working."

Albie stared angrily at Mr. Pierce. "What do you mean, it's not working? It's my emotion."

Mr. Pierce smiled patiently. "Albert, I'm sure that particular time in your life was very bleak," he said, "but it isn't working for the soliloquy. Maybe depression isn't the right approach. Maybe you need to look at it from another angle."

"Like what?"

"Let's try something. Let's take the word 'death' out of the equation and substitute 'not being.' After all, the words are 'To be, or not to be.' Hamlet must decide between being and not being. He would like to choose not being—that is, he would like 'not to be.' It would certainly be easier. However, he is so afraid of not being that he chooses the harder path. He chooses to be."

"Geez," said Albie. "I never really thought about it like that."

Mr. Pierce reached up and rubbed his eyes. "Well, think about it."

"So?" asked Maggie. "How was it?" She was sitting at the top of the back steps. The gown and the make-up were gone. She was wearing a pair of jeans and a blue workshirt.

Albie shrugged. "It started out good. Then it got bad. Then it got worse. Then it got a little better. I think."

Maggie stood up and smiled. "Where's the bodkin?" she asked.

"I left it backstage. Do you mind if I wear this?" He was still wearing the Hamlet costume—flowing white sleeves, tight black jeans, and black loafers. "Maybe it'll get me in the mood. Anyway, the dressing room's locked."

Maggie laughed and shook her head. "I don't mind."

Albie did a deep Shakespearean bow. "After you, my lady." They walked down the back stairs together, one at a time. "Geez," he said, "I don't know what to do. I mean, he gave me a few ideas, but the show's tomorrow. It's a little late now."

"Damn him," said Maggie. "He's been so busy with Cliff and their sordid little affair that he left you out on a limb."

Albie stopped and stared at her in surprise. "Do you really think they're . . . ?"

"Of course I think so," said Maggie. "Have you seen the way he looks at Cliff? And Cliff gives it right back to him. Frankly they make me a little sick."

"But what about Stephanie?"

"Stephanie's not so bad. She's been working hard on the scene."

"No, I mean, what about Stephanie and Cliff? They're all over each other during the breaks. If that's a front, they both deserve Academy Awards."

Maggie shook her head and smiled. "Have you ever heard of a bisexual?"

"Yeah, but still . . ." They were at the back doors of the school. As they stepped outside, they were hit with a blast of hot, humid air. "Geez, it's like walking underwater."

"They said it was supposed to rain."

Albie and Maggie walked along the sidewalk toward the trees. Beyond the athletic field, the sun was setting like a hoop of fire. Albie thought of reaching down and holding Maggie's hand. It would be nice, walking along behind the school, holding hands at sunset. But if he held her hand, would she hold his? *To hold, or not to hold? That is the question.*

"Maggie, how come you're so friendly with Stephanie all of a sudden?"

"What do you mean? We're doing a scene together."

Albie stopped on the sidewalk and looked out toward the sun. It was setting fast. There was just a semicircle of orange fire over the horizon. "I don't know," he said. "Maybe I'm crazy or naive or whatever, but first Cliff tells me Mr. Pierce is gay. Fine. No problem. He's a great teacher. I don't care what he does with his spare time. Then Mitch tells me that *he's* gay. Still fine. He's my friend. I accept him the way he is. Now you're telling me that Cliff is bisexual. For some reason that I can't explain, this is throwing off the fine factor. And then you and Stephanie are suddenly best buddies and, well, geez . . ."

Maggie smiled. Her face glowed in the setting sun. "I like men," she said. "Men and boys."

"What am I?" Albie asked.

Maggie looked into his eyes as if the answer were written in bold letters across his baby blues. "In-between."

When they reached the trees, Albie stepped off the sidewalk to go and get his bicycle. Maggie reached out and caught his arm from behind. "Can I see it?" she asked.

"See what?"

"Your secret place."

Albie could feel himself blushing. "Geez, I mean, it's not really any big deal. It's just a place I park my bike."

"Can I see it?"

"Sure. C'mon."

He turned and walked into the trees. It was a moment before he realized that Maggie was still holding his hand. He was right. It *was* nice. Very nice. *To hold. That is the answer.*

The tall trees blocked out the last rays of the sun. When they reached the spot where he had locked his Peugeot, it was almost dark. Albie turned to Maggie and smiled. "Well, this is it. Pretty exciting, huh?"

Maggie looked around the secret place. There wasn't much to see in the darkness. The white bicycle. The metal chain. The tall trees shielding them from the world outside. Maggie studied every corner and crevice, every shape and shadow. The green sparks in her eyes were like magic fireflies, dancing and darting in the thick humid air. "I love it," she said.

Albie pulled her toward him. He reached down and lifted her face up toward his. Then he kissed her gently on the lips. It was so natural. So easy. He wrapped his arms around her and pulled her closer. Their bodies fit together perfectly. It was so different than he had expected. So easy and warm and right. And exciting. He was breathing hard, and the jayster was pressing against his jeans. He could feel Maggie's breasts, soft and full against his chest. He unwrapped his right arm from her shoulder and slipped his hand between their bodies. They were kissing passionately—they'd never even come up for air. Very subtly, he inched his long fingers toward the buttons of her shirt. He was almost there, a little farther, a little farther . . .

"Stop that," Maggie whispered. Her lips were still

brushing his. She was breathing hard. She was excited, too.

Albie pulled his hand away, and they fell back into their kiss. The jayster was rock hard now, pressing painfully against his zipper. After a few moments, his hand began to move again. His fingers reached for Maggie's buttons. She wanted it, too. He knew she did. Closer . . . closer . . . closer . . .

Maggie broke away from their kiss. She was still in his arms, but she was no longer pressing against him. "I said stop it, Albie."

"Why?"

"It's too soon."

"We've known each other all summer."

"Not like this." She smiled sweetly and kissed him on the lips. "Isn't this enough," she whispered, "for now?"

She melted back into his arms and kissed him passionately. Albie ordered his hand to move away, but it wasn't listening—it was taking orders from the jayster. Ever so slowly, it crept toward the buttons of her shirt. It was desperate. *Do it. Do it. She wants it, too. She's just playing hard to get. Inch by inch. Closer . . . closer . . . closer . . . there! Yes!*

"No, Albie!"

He ripped her buttons.

"No!"

He reached into her blouse.

"No!"

In a single violent motion, Maggie smashed her elbows against his rib cage and kicked him hard between the legs.

"Yeoowww!"

Albie collapsed in a heap on the ground. He was gasping for breath and clutching his crotch. The jayster was dead. His balls were crushed. Maggie stood above him, holding her shirt together. The green sparks in her eyes were like an electric bodkin searching for his heart.

"Damn you, Albie," she whispered. "I thought you were special." Then she disappeared.

17

For a long time, Albie lay on the ground, staring into the dark circle of sky above the trees. The pain between his legs was like a chain saw ripping through his vital organs. But the pain in his heart was worse. He had done it. Permanently. Forever. He had blown it with Maggie. No, it was worse. Maggie hated him.

Albie sat up and tried to breathe slowly and evenly. It was bad enough with his shattered jayster, but his ribs felt like they were broken. On top of that, the air was so thick it was hard to breathe anyway. *It'll probably rain*, he thought. *Great. Maybe I can stay here and drown.*

Finally, he staggered to his feet. It was a slow painful process, but he wasn't in a hurry. He leaned on his Peugeot, opened the lock, and pulled the chain from around the big tree. He dragged it through the spokes and wrapped it around the seat stem. Then he wheeled the 12-speed out of the secret place. There was no way he could ride. His crotch was history.

He walked the bike around toward the front of the school. There were rows and rows of bicycle racks—neat and empty and shiny in the dim light of the streetlamps. Albie rolled his Peugeot into a slot in one of the racks. He didn't bother to lock it. As he walked away, he passed the spot on the main sidewalk where he had puked up the bologna and whiskey. *Ah! Those were the good old days.*

He hobbled up the hill toward the railroad tracks. When he reached the top, he paused and looked back down the hill toward the secret spot. His voice was quiet and real. "You practically raped her, asshole."

Albie walked east toward downtown Wilmont. He didn't know why—it was just somewhere to walk. He was moving a little easier now. The pain between his legs had become a dull, throbbing ache. He could live with that. What he couldn't live with was his life.

The downtown streets were completely deserted. All the stores were closed. At the main intersection, there was a bank with a flashing electric sign. In bright lights it said: 10:33 TIME TO START SAVING. Then it said: 95°F. Then it said: 10:34. Then it said: 35°C.

There was a telephone booth across the street from the bank. He walked over, stepped inside, and reached into his pocket for change. All he had was a five-dollar bill; Hamlet didn't carry change. He pushed zero and waited for the operator. "I'd like to make a collect call from Albie." After a few moments, his mother came on the line. "Hi, Mom . . . Yeah, I know it's late . . . it's 10:34 . . . Yeah, we just finished . . . you know how it is with a dress rehearsal . . . We took a dinner break . . . No, don't wait up. Mitch and I are gonna get a pizza . . . I won't . . . Okay. 'Bye.''

Albie hung up the phone and let out a long, deep breath. "Be yourself," he said. "Rape women and lie to your mother.'' He stepped out of the telephone booth and looked down the street. It was absolutely dead. The air was so humid that he felt like he was standing in a rainstorm without the rain. His eyes were burning from sweat, and he could taste salt in his mouth. His white shirt was drenched—sweat was even dripping into his underwear.

He continued walking east. When he reached the lakefront, he crossed the grassy strip and looked out over the water. It was perfectly still. Glass. Not a hint of a wave. Not a breath of a breeze. The lake was dead. *Not to be.*

Albie walked north along the grass. It was the wrong direction if he were going home, but he wasn't going home. Not yet, anyway. He just wanted to walk. The pain wasn't as bad if he kept moving. He looked around for kids making out or having a good time. They were usually sitting at the picnic tables or out on the rocks or maybe on the sand. But there was nobody. Absolutely nobody.

The grass ended at Cliff's beach. It was completely empty. No lifeguards. No Cliff. No girl in green. He climbed over the wooden fence and walked across the sand. Suddenly, his legs felt tired and rubbery. With the thick humid air, it was like walking on the bottom of the ocean. He flopped down on his belly and rested.

As he lay on his stomach, he thought back to his first performance as a salamander. He could still see the crowded audition room, the students against the walls and beneath the windows—there was more oxygen by the windows. He could see Mr. Pierce behind his little table. He could hear Mitch's jokes and Cliff's challenge.

What you really mean, Albie, is do I think you'll *make it.*

He could remember the late lamented jayster popping up at the curves under Stephanie's blouse. He could feel the cold, hard linoleum and taste the bitter suede of Mr. Pierce's hush puppies. The only one he couldn't remember was Maggie. She was there. She had to be. But he couldn't remember. She was gone completely. Erased.

"I was better off then," he said aloud. "Pierce knew it all along. I'm a lousy Hamlet, but I'm one hell of a salamander."

Instinctively, he began to slither across the sand. It was so easy after his long walk, so natural. When he reached the wet sand at the edge of the lake, he found himself surrounded by dead, rotting fish. It was disgusting, even for a salamander. So he slithered toward the rocks on the north end of the beach. He pulled himself onto the first rock and slithered across its hard uneven surface. It hurt a little, but he was beyond pain. Anyway, he deserved whatever he got. The jayster was dead. Long live the salamander!

Albie pulled himself over the second rock and the third and the fourth. It wasn't so bad really, once he got the hang of it. There were endless shapes and sides and

crevices and indentations. Rocks were made for salamanders. Next he passed a private beach. That was easy.
He just slithered down on the sand and whipped right
through it. Salamanders liked beaches, too.

After a while, the slithering took its toll. His white
Hamlet shirt was ripped to shreds, and his tight black
jeans were torn at the knees. His loafers were scraped
beyond salvation. There were patches of blood on his
elbows and knees and smaller nicks and cuts on his face.
His entire body was caked with sand and sweat. But the
worst part was the air—there wasn't any. Albie picked
out a nice flat rock and curled into a salamander sleeping
position. Then he closed his eyes.

When he woke up, the sky was gray. Albie lifted his
head a few inches from the rock. "What am I doing on
a rock?" he asked. "Oh, yeah. That."

He sat up and looked out at the lake. The water
was completely still, and a thick haze hung over the
surface. There was a slight glow in the deepest reaches
of the haze. It wouldn't be much of a sunrise. On the
other side of the rocks, there was a thin strip of sand and
a grove of tall elm trees. Albie slipped down from the
rock and stretched. His whole body ached.

He walked north along the narrow strip of beach.
He was starving. He hadn't eaten any dinner, and all
that walking and slithering had worked up an appetite.
After twenty or thirty steps, he came to an opening. The
beach widened to the right, and there was an enormous
mansion to the left. A smile crept over his face—it was
Brent's house. He looked back toward the rocks. Maybe

he'd slept on the rock where he made out with Stephanie. *Could be,* he thought. *It's possible. But who the hell cares?*

He walked around the side of the house to the long gravel driveway and out onto the street. There weren't many cars—it was too early for morning rush hour.

"So, Mr. Salamander," he asked, "who's serving breakfast?"

There weren't any cozy cafes on the north side of town. Of course, he could always go home, but he wasn't ready for that. His best bet was over near the high school. There had to be something open.

As he walked toward the school, Albie passed the huge houses of the north side. He remembered riding in Cliff's car, watching them pass in the afternoon sun. They had seemed like something from another world. They still did. Long, curving driveways stretched from the street toward hidden entranceways. Tall wrought-iron fences protected them from scum like him. Every once in a while, he passed a maid or gardener arriving early for work. They gave him some pretty strange looks.

By the time he reached the school, it was almost sunrise. It was amazing how it could be so light, and yet the sun wasn't actually up. "It's the light from the edge of the world," he said out loud. He didn't know if it was right, but it sounded pretty good. None of the places on the north side were open, so he walked toward the south, along the front sidewalk of the school. The heat and humidity were even worse than during the night. If it didn't rain soon, the sky was going to explode.

His Peugeot was right where he had left it, in the bicycle rack by the front entrance. Albie stopped a few feet away and gazed at it as though he were seeing it for the first time. Nothing was really different—it was the same bike. But it was out in the open. All night. And it had survived.

Albie wiped the sweat off his hands with what was left of his Hamlet shirt and rolled the bike out of the slot. Then, very carefully, he eased himself onto the hard leather seat. "Yeoww!" It was still pretty sore down there. He pulled off his shirt and wadded it into a cushion. That was an improvement. He slipped the bike into low gear and pedaled toward the railroad tracks.

As he glided over the top of the hill, Albie saw the Burger Chief, his painted face and feathered warbonnet floating high above the buildings. He seemed like a guardian angel watching over the town and the school. Watching over Albie, too. Maybe. If there was one hopeless case in Wilmont, it was probably Albie. "Mr. Not-to-be," he said. "That's me."

Suddenly Albie had a vision of a Chiefburger. Thick and juicy with mustard, tomato, and onions. A large order of onion rings and a strawberry shake. That's what he wanted last night—before he went berserk and mauled Maggie. That's what he wanted now. It was the perfect breakfast. The only solution.

"Screw *Hamlet*. I'll trade my kingdom for a Chiefburger." He turned off the main road and pedaled toward the Chief.

It didn't look very promising. The diner was dark and there weren't any cars in the parking lot. He leaned his bicycle against the giant moccasin and went over to the window. Nothing. No sign of life. No sign of a Chiefburger.

"Not to be."

He walked back over to his bike and sat down on the giant moccasin. His stomach was churning; he was starving and exhausted. He took a deep breath of the humid air, closed his eyes, and leaned back against the Chief's leg. He could still see the Chiefburger in his mind. Thick. Juicy. Succulent. Satisfying. He took another breath, opened his eyes, and looked up toward the sky. There it was, thirty-five feet above him—the biggest, thickest, juiciest Chiefburger in the world. It had been waiting for him all along, right there in the Chief's hand.

Albie stood up on the moccasin and placed his hands on the giant leg. It wouldn't be easy. He was tired and hungry and slick with sweat. But it was do or die. To be, or not to be. Right here. Right now. He grabbed his Hamlet shirt and wiped the sweat off his body. Then he wrapped his long arms around the Chief's calf and pressed his knees against the ankles. Slowly he began to shimmy up the leg, a few inches at a time, pulling with his arms and pushing with his knees. It was just like climbing a tree, except there weren't any branches to help him.

When he reached the Chief's knee, he pulled himself onto the kneecap and rested for a minute. He was already breathing heavily in the damp heat. The thigh was much bigger than the calf—the Chief had some major muscles. Albie reached around the quadriceps and pulled himself upward. It was slow going, but he made it to the bottom of the breechcloth. The folds in the cloth gave him a little leverage as he worked himself up toward the Chief's waist.

The top of the breechcloth was a narrow ledge. Albie pulled himself up and rested again. He looked down at his Peugeot, leaning comfortably against the moccasin. It was smaller than he remembered it. He was about twenty-five feet above the ground. The giant burger was about ten feet above him and fifteen feet out, sitting seductively in the Chief's palm. From his perch on the breechcloth, it looked enormous.

"Well, Mr. Hamlet, what's the plan?"

He gazed up the Chief's broad, muscular chest to his giant armpit. There was no way he was going to shimmy straight up his chest. There was nothing to hold onto. He could stand on the ledge and reach for the armpit, but he wouldn't be able to get a grip on the arm. The best bet was the elbow. It was about eight feet out from the breechcloth ledge. He would have to jump, but it was definitely possible. Anything was possible.

Albie stood on the ledge and leaned back against the Chief's rib cage. He looked down at his Peugeot and the moccasin and the hard edge of the parking lot. He looked up at the giant burger and followed the Chief's forearm to the crook in the elbow, waiting for him like a safe harbor. He took a deep breath, closed his eyes, and pictured four plastic chairs clattering to the ground. Relaxation. He took another breath and imagined the little black wheels on Mr. Pierce's tie. Concentration. He breathed again and listened to Maggie's words. *Damn you, Albie. I thought you were special.* Memory. The three steps. The Method.

"To be, or not to be!" he cried.

Then he jumped.

The next thing he knew, he was sitting on top of the giant Chiefburger, looking out over the town. It was beautiful and peaceful with its elm trees and houses and streets and sidewalks. He could see the railroad tracks running across the little hill. He could see the school with its buildings and wings and annexes. He could see the rows of bicycle racks in the front and the broad, open athletic field in the back. He could even see the secret place—a grove of trees and a tiny black hole.

As Albie gazed at the world below, the first golden rays of the sun erupted on the eastern horizon. To the west, there was a flash of lightning and the deep rumble of thunder. A moment later, it began to rain. Clean, cool, soothing rain. Albie sat on the Chiefburger and turned his face upward toward the sky, smiling and laughing as the water ran over his body.

"To be!" he shouted.

18

ALBIE ROLLED HIS Peugeot into one of the bike racks in front of the school. He uncoiled the long chain, threaded it through the front wheel, wrapped it around the metal bars of the rack, and pulled it through the frame. He was finished with the secret place, but he wasn't going to leave his bike unlocked. There were limits.

He walked in the entrance and headed down the first-floor hallway toward the back stairs. He was carrying what was left of his Hamlet costume in a knapsack. It was a total disaster, but that was perfect. In fact, it was exactly what he had in mind. Luckily his mother had never seen it—she had enough to worry about. He'd slipped into the apartment and cleaned up while she was still asleep. By the time she woke up, he was under the covers and out like a light.

He reached the bottom of the stairs and started climbing, one at a time. He was still pretty exhausted. He'd slept all day, but that salamandering had taken its toll. He'd be all right by showtime, though. The adrenalin would start pumping and those lights would shine and . . . He stopped at the second-floor landing and looked up the stairs. He couldn't see anyone, but there were voices echoing down the staircase. It was Cliff and Mr. Pierce.

Albie climbed a few more steps. He could hear more clearly now. If he stretched forward and looked up the next flight of stairs, he could just see them. Cliff was standing at the top of the stairs, pacing back and forth— a few steps right, a few steps left. Mr. Pierce was standing a step below.

"Please, Clifford," he said. "We'll go for a drink."

"No, Dale. I'm sorry."

"Are you saying it's over?"

"It never was."

Mr. Pierce reached out and grabbed the banister for support. "It's me, isn't it? I'm old and ugly."

Cliff stopped pacing and smiled at Mr. Pierce. "You're brilliant, Dale. And you're not ugly at all."

"It's Stephanie."

Cliff shook his head. "It has nothing to do with Stephanie."

"Then what? I need to understand."

"I thought we could be friends."

"We are friends."

"You want more."

"No, Clifford . . . really . . ."

"I'm sorry, Dale. It's me. It's just me." Cliff turned and disappeared down the hall. Using the banister for support, Mr. Pierce crumpled slowly into a sitting position. His head dropped into his hands.

Suddenly, Albie felt embarrassed to be watching. This was a private life. It wasn't a scene on a stage. He turned to go back down the stairs, but as he pivoted on his size twelve feet, his knapsack scraped against the banister. Mr. Pierce looked down at him. His voice was gentle. "Albert, you're early."

"Uh, yes, sir. I just got here. Just this very second, actually. This very millisecond."

"How nice," said Mr. Pierce. He wasn't really listening.

Albie climbed the rest of the stairs. When he reached the top, Mr. Pierce looked up and said, "We're lucky."

Albie sat down beside him. "Lucky, sir?"

"A student like Clifford appears so rarely. The talent. Looks. Personality. We're lucky to have him."

"I think we're lucky to have you."

Mr. Pierce smiled slightly. His eyes looked bloodshot. "Thank you, Albert. That's very kind. But it's a load of crap."

"You're a great teacher. You studied with Strasberg, for God's sake."

Mr. Pierce shook his head and gazed through Albie into a world of his own imagination. It was the blacked-out-window look. "I never studied with Strasberg."

"What are you talking about? Of course you did. You were an actor in New York and everything."

He rubbed his eyes and stared deeper into the past.

"Yes, Albert. I was an actor in New York. And I wanted to study the Method more than I wanted to eat. But I wasn't accepted at the Studio. I wasn't good enough."

Albie dragged his fingernails along the protective material of his knapsack. Then he slowly crumpled the knapsack in his hands. It would wrinkle the costume, but it didn't matter. It was perfect anyway.

"I don't care," he said. "You're a great teacher. That's good enough."

Albie stood in the right wing, peering out from behind the old musty curtain. The seats were filling up quickly. About half the people were teachers and drama students; the other half were parents and families. His mother was sitting with Roger in the second row, holding the program close to her eyes and reading carefully. She looked very pretty. No sad, tired smiles. No dumb questions. Actually, she was a heck of a mother.

"How's it look?" Mitch stood behind him, whispering into his ear.

Albie turned and whispered back. "I think it's gonna be a full house."

"What the hell happened to your costume?" Mitch stared at Albie's Hamlet costume. The white flowing shirt was ripped to shreds, the tight black pants had giant holes in the knees, and the black loafers were so scraped up that they looked like gray loafers. The bodkin still looked pretty good.

"I was a salamander," Albie said. "Then I climbed the Burger Chief."

"You what?" Mitch asked loudly.

"Shhhh!" Albie whispered. "I climbed the Burger Chief. It was easy. I just started at the moccasin and . . ."

"I don't want to hear about it," said Mitch. "You're insane and we have a show in ten minutes and I just don't want to hear about it."

"Geez, what if I didn't want to hear about it in the ice-cream parlor?"

Mitch looked down at the wooden boards of the stage. "You're right," he said. "I do want to hear about it. But right now, I need to concentrate." He took a step closer and wrapped his arms around Albie. "Break a leg."

Albie encircled Mitch with his own arms. "You, too." They held each other silently. Albie could feel Mitch's breathing and smell the tobacco on his breath. For an instant, he thought he heard the beating of his heart. But that was impossible—it was only his imagination. Finally, as if by a secret signal, they released each other and walked away.

Albie peeked around the edge of the curtain. The house was almost full. Students were standing along the back wall and over by the windows. He focused on an empty seat in the last row, in front of the lightboard. It belonged to Mr. Pierce. Albie hadn't seen him since the back stairs. Maybe he was busy with something for the show. Maybe he wasn't. Either way, Albie was worried. Mr. Pierce could be pretty nasty, but he was a great teacher. He deserved to be happy.

Albie stepped away from the curtain and peered across the stage. Cliff and Stephanie were waiting in the other wing, holding hands and standing as close as possible. Stephanie looked dynamite in her Anastasia gown. It was just a white dress with some rhinestones around the collar, but she made the most of it. Cliff looked pretty funny in his hobo costume. *It's true*, Albie thought. *These royal women go for bums. No, that's not fair. Cliff's no bum.*

Of course, the real issue on the other side of the stage wasn't Cliff and Stephanie. And it sure as heck wasn't Brent. It was Maggie. She was standing by herself, getting into her role as the Dowager Empress. Even though she was supposed to be an old lady, she was beautiful in her green gown. Albie hadn't spoken a word to her since the secret place. She passed him as she walked across the stage, but she was with Stephanie. Stephanie said, "Hi." Maggie just looked away. He didn't blame her.

The houselights began to dim and the audience grew quiet. Maggie and Stephanie got into place for *Anastasia*. Albie peeked around the curtain to see if Mr. Pierce had made it, but the house was too dark. The only illumination was the tiny light on the lightboard, shining on the cues. Albie could hear the stagehand breathing beside him. It was curtain time.

"Let's go," whispered the stagehand.

"Just a second," Albie whispered. He was staring into the darkness, trying desperately to see Mr. Pierce's seat. How could he do *Hamlet* without Mr. Pierce? He had to be there.

"C'mon, Albie."

Albie was about to step back into the wing when he saw a tall, thin figure pass in front of the lightboard. "Now," he whispered.

The curtain opened and the lights came up. Maggie was seated downstage left on a small couch. Stephanie stood upstage right. The rhinestones around her collar sparkled like diamonds in the lights. That was the illusion of the stage. Maggie wasn't wearing rhinestones, but the green sparks in her eyes reflected the light like precious stones. That wasn't an illusion.

The Dowager Empress looked at Anastasia with regal disdain. Slowly, methodically, she examined her from head to toe as if she were a statue in a museum. Finally, she turned her head away, ever so slightly. "Yes," she said, "I can see why the others have believed, especially my romantic-minded nephew. The likeness is good enough for a waxwork gallery."

As the scene progressed, Albie could feel himself drawn into the heart of the Empress. Was Anastasia an imposter? Or was she the only surviving daughter of Czar Nicholas II? As the Empress wavered, he wavered. As she struggled with the truth, he struggled, too. He peeked around the edge of the curtain into the dark house. The audience was absolutely silent. He could feel their concentration.

When the scene ended, the entire house erupted in applause. There were even a few bravos. The actors in the wings applauded, too. Maggie and Stephanie took a quick bow at the center of the stage and stepped off into the left wing. Then the lights went dark and the stagehands set up for the next scene.

In *A Taste of Honey*, Jennifer played Jo, a young English girl who is pregnant and abandoned. Scott played Geof, a gay boy who befriends her. As the lights came up, they walked onto the stage as if they were entering Jo's apartment. Jo flopped onto the couch and let out a long deep sigh.

"Let me lie here and don't wake me up for a month."

Geof reached for an imaginary light switch. "Shall I put the light on?" he asked.

"No. Don't you dare put that light on." Jennifer was a natural for the part. She was tough and vulnerable at the same time.

"Did you enjoy the fair?" Scott was definitely not a natural. He wasn't embarrassing or anything, but he wasn't gay. *What is gay?* Albie didn't know. He would probably never know. But, whatever it was, Scott didn't have it.

Albie looked across the stage at Maggie. If he could only make eye contact, even for a split second, he would feel a little better. There were giant butterflies floating around in his stomach. Every word spoken on the stage brought him that much closer to *Hamlet*. He wasn't wavering. He'd made his decision. He knew exactly what he was going to do. But a smile from Maggie would anchor him. Of course there was nothing. What did he expect? She was busy watching the scene. And besides, he was a total jerk.

When the scene was over, Jennifer and Scott took their bows at the center of the stage. The applause was strong and steady, but it wasn't like the reaction to *Anastasia*. Albie took a few deep breaths. The butterflies were multiplying. He was nauseated. He was exhausted. He couldn't remember his lines. He considered walking down the wooden steps and disappearing into the night. Then he remembered the Burger Chief. No. He had a vision. He had to live with it.

The lights went dark and Jennifer and Scott slipped into the right wing. The stagehands quickly cleared the stage. No couch for *Hamlet*—just the empty boards. Albie walked across the stage toward the other side. It didn't matter where he made his entrance. Nothing really mattered except the concept. He couldn't see Maggie in the darkness, but he made a quick guess and whispered, "I'm sorry."

He guessed right. "You should be," she whispered.

"I am. I love you."

The lights came up. He flopped on his belly and began to slither onto the stage. "To be, or not to be, that is the question." He could feel the hard wood of the boards beneath his body. Sharp slivers pierced his hands and knees. His face was inches above the stage. "Whether 'tis nobler in the mind to suffer the slings and arrows of outrageous fortune or to take arms against a sea of troubles, and by opposing end them. To die—to sleep—no more."

He was at the center of the stage now, still slithering on his belly. His snakelike tail undulated behind him, and his beady amphibian eyes searched the empty stage for prey. He could hear whispers in the audience. Even laughter here and there. But he didn't care. He was inside it for better or worse. He was a salamander Hamlet.

"To sleep—perchance to dream: ay, there's the rub!" Albie began to rise from his belly. First into a push-up position, then onto all fours like a dog. But he wasn't a dog. He was a salamander growing, lifting himself from the ground by the force of his will to be.

"For who would bear the whips and scorns of time, the oppressor's wrong, the proud man's contumely, the pangs of despised love . . ." He was standing on two legs now, his back bent like an old man carrying a heavy burden. But he wasn't an old man. He was a salamander choosing to be.

"When he himself might his quietus make with a bare bodkin?" The bodkin was in his tiny amphibian hand, holding him down with its weight. Slowly, his hand grew out around the knife. It was no longer the hand of a salamander. It was the long-fingered hand of a man. He paused in the soliloquy and looked at the bodkin as if he were seeing it for the first time. It was so tiny really, so insignificant in the hand of a man. Then he tossed the knife to the back of the stage like a child who no longer needed his toy.

"Who would these fardels bear, to grunt and sweat under a weary life . . ." He continued the soliloquy, straightening his body with every word. It was painful, ever so painful, but every movement brought him closer to being . . . being . . . being. He had made his choice. He would bear these fardels. He was a salamander becoming a man. A man who had once been a salamander. He was growing, growing, growing, until finally he stood at his full height, a tall Hamlet, his spine straight, his head erect, his ragged costume hanging proudly on his 6'3" frame. He looked to the left wing and gazed directly into Maggie's eyes. "Soft you now!" he cried. "The fair Ophelia!"

The theater was silent for a moment. Then the

applause began. It started with Mitch, laughing and clapping and shouting at the same time. The other actors picked it up. Cliff was roaring, "Big guy! Big guy!" It spread into the house, first the front rows, then along the blacked-out windows and toward the back, growing and growing until it echoed throughout the theater. Mr. Pierce cried, "Bravo! Bravo!" and others joined the cry. There were shouts and whistles and people on their feet.

It was an actor's dream, but Albie never saw it. He stood downstage left, still gazing at Maggie, the fair Ophelia. She was the only one in the entire theater who wasn't clapping. Her face was serious and the green sparks in her eyes glowed in the shadows of the wing. *Please*, Albie thought. *Please*. And then her face began to change. Slowly, ever so slowly. As slowly as a salamander becomes a man, Maggie smiled.